THE LAST LEADER

To my wife, Melissa

PUBLISHED BY MOODY HOUSE LLC
WWW.MOODY.HOUSE

First Edition: *April 14, 2019*
Seventeenth Print Run: *January 25, 2021*
ISBN-13: 978-0692082782

What if women ruled the world?

It was all made possible by technology. The first big step was the washing machine, freeing housewives from the previously brutal process of getting those grass stains out. Soon after, they claimed the right to vote.

The next moment arrived when Rosie the Riveter led a generation of women into factories, assembling the heavy metals of World War II. Then came the dishwasher, the microwave, and factories that started making frozen dinners instead of bombs ... no more hours spent whipping up dinner from scratch.

Suddenly, there was all this extra time. While some women spent it shopping and watching the flurry of soap operas saturating the airwaves, others became hyper-educated. With the dawn of the Web, this accelerated rate of learning went worldwide, and suddenly women were sometimes as smart as men, but usually smarter.

Then came all the wireless wonders, self-driving cars, holograms and finally androids. The stage was set for the final ascent of womankind, long foreseen by ancient sages who understood world cycles.

The children of tomorrow will know **Emperia Bloom**, or someone a lot like her. She represents the culmination of the "feminine shift" in world consciousness, fierce at first to match the aggressive level of masculine energies.

Caught in the middle of the paradigm shift is **Phoenix Flynn**, representing the average downcast man in a society ruled by powerful women. Strong, smart yet soft-spoken, could he be the one to bring balance?

THE LAST LEADER

BY JOE MOODY

ACT 1

1

Her name was Morgan, queen of the teenage guy's dream. In the blood-bathed streets on the fierce side of town, she strutted. Fear didn't mix in the cocktail she sipped from a water bottle on the cable car that dropped her at 12th and Vine. The secrets of the city rising out of the fog on the edge of civilization were hers to keep.

She approached Phoenix, just another guy trying to make it in a society ruled by badass women. He learned early to keep his place: avoid eye contact, speak only when spoken to, *yield*... But something gripped his brain as he watched this Morgan character.

She headed down the sidewalk toward where he stood, steely eyes fixed on him, expecting him to get out of her way.

But he didn't.

He couldn't this time, without knowing why.

So, she ran right into him, bumping her shoulder against him forcefully. The impact knocked him back more than he expected. She laughed and read the name embroidered in gold on the pocket of his gray mechanic's shirt. "Phoenix, huh?"

He shook his head, about to turn away, when she recited an ancient passage...

"His gaze expresses righteousness.

His tongue utters sincerity.

His ears enjoy music.

His spurs overpower transgressors."

She winked knowingly. "So it is written of The Phoenix."

He stared at her, bewildered beneath his auburn hair, blue eyes gleaming. "How'd you remember all that?"

"I remember everything," she said, swinging her bob-cut brown hair to the side. And without another word, she marched forward in her leather pants and vest, boot heels thumping.

"What's your name?" he called out, trying to keep up.

She stopped. "I'll give you more than that, if you have what it takes to go all the way." She smiled wickedly. "... into the fire."

He scoffed. "You're messed up."

Morgan glared through him. "And when illusion burns in a flash, The Phoenix will rise anew from the ash."

Her words struck an inner chord, notes he never knew.

"Come on, if you dare," she said, leading him down an alley. A rational voice inside his mind urged him to turn back, but he ignored it. He craved to glimpse the kind of world that put the force in her fiery step.

Arriving at a rusty metal gate, a sign declared, *Stay out. Hazardous.* Morgan swung it open.

Phoenix tried to be nonchalant as he followed her through the entrance, but as she slammed the gate behind them, he felt a chill go up his neck.

Smoke lingered in the air as they stepped into the courtyard, lush with greenery and ivy crawling up brick walls. A pathway of mossy stones led to a husky woman puffing a cigar, holding back a giant, growling bullmastiff with a flimsy leather leash. She looked at Phoenix with a wry smile. "Why's a sweet guy like you hanging out with Morgan?"

Before Phoenix could respond, Morgan grabbed his arm. "It's our first date."

The woman took a puff with a skeptical look in her eyes. "Well, you're just in time for the revolution." She pulled open a steel door on the brick building. Music of a roadhouse piano spilled into the courtyard.

"Escort me," said Morgan, and Phoenix led her into a dark vestibule lined with mahogany panels. Noticing him slouching, she scolded him. "Shoulders back. Be confident, like a *true* phoenix."

Walking in rhythm to the music, they passed through a velvet curtained doorway into a club. The rich vintage décor and women dancing like flapper girls near a piano evoked a *Roaring Twenties* speakeasy.

A snare drum fired up, adding a backbone to the piano that belted out a raucous version of *Stars and Stripes Forever*. Morgan and Phoenix swayed as they walked. She leaned out to spin around him, then pulled herself close to shoot him a dark stare.

As the piano played on, a man approached Morgan. His gruff voice spoke with a tinge of sarcasm. "Save me the last dance." A man stepped into the light, in his mid-thirties with a sun-baked face and handlebar mustache, clothes heavily worn like a drifter who goes more by whim than plan.

"What are you doing here, Halzac?" said Morgan.

"Not your concern, dear."

Halzac spoke aside to Phoenix. "Careful, man. She takes what she wants, then vanishes like smoke."

A smiling, zippy blond appeared at the table. "What can I get you guys?"

"A pitcher of ale," said Halzac, pointing at Morgan. "On her."

Morgan paused, then nodded at the waitress to approve the order.

The music stopped as a man in a velvet smoking jacket took the stage. His black goatee complemented his ebony complexion. Waving his hand, he waited for the clamor to die down. "Something's happening here." He pointed over at a holographic television above the bar area.

The words *Breaking News: President to announce new voting system* faded to a live scene from the Pink House. Formerly known as the White House, the newly redesigned power center was a testimonial to the relentless sway of a magnetic young president: Emperia Bloom.

The camera focused on Emperia, statuesque on the Truman Balcony, looking down upon the crowd. Shimmering, black locks framed her porcelain face, showing the blend of her Asian father and Californian mother. Every gesture and turn of her head exuded a confidence that defied her youth. Her black silk suit declared strength while the golden trim spoke of beauty. A red, white and blue crown of roses adorned her hair, pulled back by a golden eagle pin.

Her voice, commanding yet melodic, quieted both the live

crowd and those in the club watching her hologram.

"The stars are out," she said, staring skyward, traces like crushed diamond flashing around her coal-black eyes. "I like to remind myself every day how lucky we are, in this land of life, liberty and the pursuit of good shoes." She winked to some laughter.

"And how far we've come. In fact, just today the Make-Yourself-Useful program reached ten million men strong. Thanks to Man's renewed focus on service, bridges are newer, roads are freshly paved, and urban infrastructures are revitalized. Women, we guided them well. In fact, that Shining City on the Hill never shined brighter!" The cheers included whistles and barking hollers.

"I'd also like to thank our beloved androids: the MotorMaidens who police our streets with elegant force, and the Emperial Robots – our formidable Embots – who keep the peace inside and outside our borders. Together, you relieve men of their most dangerous tasks, and give women new muscle. We salute you!" A robotic, high-pitched, whirring noise filled the air, sounding more eerie than celebratory.

"But there's another matter I must address tonight." The camera closed in on her face. "Our precious voting system, the foundation of freedom, has been hacked in multiple states. It's a problem we can no longer ignore. Therefore, I am proceeding with plans to create a new unified voting system."

As cheers erupted, the TV turned off. The man stroked his goatee, pacing up and down the stage. "Emperia Bloom. What can we say? She dazzles, dizzies the opposition. She swapped our soldiers for bots and everybody clapped. Now, she wants control of the vote. '*Hackers*,' she says. But what if *she's* the hacker?"

7

The club remained quiet. "Tomorrow morning, we'll be diggin' deeper, talkin' solutions, constitutions, revolutions..." He raised a glass of beer. "Until then, to freedom!" People cheered and whistled as the band kicked into the *Star-Spangled Banner*.

Phoenix shook his head. "Ah, this really isn't my scene. I happen to be one of the ten million schmucks who work for Emperia." He looked down at his LifeWatch, the federally funded wonder that tracked his work hours, vital signs and location. "This isn't looking good for my service review in the morning."

Halzac looked at Phoenix's uniform. "Emperial mechanic, huh? You must drive an Emperial truck..."

"So?"

"What makes your truck act like a buddy, that's the work of Emperia's father. Why do you think he named her Emperia? They're both trying to turn America into their own empire."

"Whatever," interrupted Morgan.

"Using friendly robots," continued Halzac. "The new opium of the masses. And the cream-of-the-crop is what's being called a *Fembot*."

Phoenix chuckled. "Fembot?"

"A beautiful-woman-bot with no social security number to do her dirty work."

Morgan shook her head. "I'll believe it when I see her."

"You'll never see her, that's the point," said Halzac.

The waitress returned with the beer. Phoenix noticed her ring: a golden sun and silver moon around an Earth-like opal.

The waitress saw Phoenix staring. "*Balance*," she said.

8

"The sun and moon balance the planet. Male and female energies balance people." She set down three mugs and a pitcher. "If one side gets out of whack, things fall apart." With that she swooped over to another table.

As Phoenix pondered her statement, Halzac lifted the pitcher of beer like it was his own giant mug and swilled out of it, his mustache soaking in the foam as he chugged.

"Damn, dude," said Phoenix, pushing his empty mug away.

A redhead on heels tromped by them. "Brenda?" said Halzac, following in her wake with pitcher in hand.

"Thank goddess, he's finally gone," said Morgan as her LifeRing began to glow. The ruby gemstone, set in gold, pulsated in a deep red hue. Like Phoenix's watch, her ring performed hundreds of functions, with a simple yet elegant design by Emperia herself.

"You work for her too?" said Phoenix.

Morgan looked up grimly. "Well, Phoenix, are you really looking for adventure? Or wanna call it a night?"

"Um, how about adventure."

"Even if it means the Phoenix you are now will no longer exist?"

"You're sounding crazy again."

She pressed down on his hand. Her metallic-gray eyes seemed to spin. "If you stay, there's no going back to who you were, like when Adam bit the apple. Are you in or out?"

Phoenix didn't like where she was going with this, but he couldn't just walk away now. He knew he'd regret it. "I'm in."

"Okay. Listen. Embots are about to bust this place, but I'm going to give you a running start." Morgan lifted the LifeRing to her lips.

"Wait, what?" said Phoenix, already regretting his decision.

She ignored him, speaking calmly into her ring. "Target clear."

A loud whirring noise shook the room, breaking glass, throwing everyone into a fury. A robotic voice blared out. "All present are under arrest for suspicion of sedition. Resistance will be met with force."

"Let's go!" yelled Morgan as she tugged Phoenix with surprising force. He landed against her chest as she locked eyes with him. "Time to fly." She pulled him behind the bar and headed for a doorway.

People scrambled in every direction as Embots flooded the club. Their skeletal frames made them light and fast, while their skull-like faces gave them a fear factor intended to prevent skirmishes before they began. Their dark eyes contained lenses powerful enough to read the date on a dime on the moon.

Morgan and Phoenix ran into the kitchen, pushing open an emergency door leading to a stairway. "Faster!" she yelled as they charged up several flights of stairs. When they reached the top, Phoenix pushed on the metal door, but it was jammed. Morgan side-kicked it like a martial artist, popping it open.

"Halt or die!" the mechanized voice of an Embot bellowed from below as its feet pounded the stairs.

Phoenix slammed the door behind them as they made it onto the roof. He grabbed a rusty cart and wedged it against the door. "Yeah, that'll stop 'em," Morgan teased. "There's a ladder on the west ledge. Good luck, Phoenix. You'll need it!" She ran to the edge of the roof and dived off, seemingly falling several stories onto the concrete sidewalk.

Phoenix ran to the edge of the building and looked for her, but only saw an orange GutterBot, claws extending from its crab-like body as it cleared leaves from a sewage drain. Law enforcement vehicles flashed colorful lights around the corner, but there was no trace of Morgan, this character who so quickly upended his regular world.

The Embot slammed against the stairway door, each strike with increasing force. The cart pried against the door bought some time, but Phoenix knew that wouldn't last. He felt a gnawing feeling in his gut, figuring it was time to turn himself in, to trust the powers-that-be would conclude he had nothing to do with any rebellion. He stood like the model employee he was trained to be. But then he realized if he could only escape, maybe tomorrow he could wake up like nothing happened.

In that same instant, the Embot rammed the door open with its shoulder, sending the cart flying. Phoenix ran to the western ledge, using his LifeWatch as a flashlight to find the ladder Morgan mentioned. After a frantic search, he spotted the top of the ladder peaking out from the ledge.

He climbed on and scrambled down a few rungs, but the ladder creaked loudly, ready to break off the wall. Phoenix froze, not realizing the bot was already directly above him, laser rifle drawn. Phoenix looked up, so startled he nearly fell off the ladder. He played off his own fear to try to gain sympathy. "Hey, I know this looks bad, but I'm an Emperial employee in good standing. I have nothing to do with any sedition." He tried to catch his breath. "And I think this ladder is about to collapse..." He reached up toward the machine like it was his lifeline.

The bot assessed the situation. "You are under arrest. Remain still for body-scan." One of the Embot's eyes popped out of the socket. Held by a flexible cable, it lowered toward Phoenix and peered at him like the disembodied eye of a cyclops.

At that moment, Phoenix had a most rebellious thought.

It all happened in an instant.

As the bot leaned over the ledge to complete the scan, Phoenix grabbed the cable that held the eye. Using all his strength, he yanked to pull the bot off balance. The bulky beast tried to resist, but gravity was on Phoenix's side. The bot wavered for a moment, then plunged off the roof's edge.

The Embot whirled through the air and crashed on the street in a sparkling finale.

Phoenix hurried down the rusty rungs and leapt to the ground. The bot lay scattered in pieces, smoldering on the street. "Internal system error... Internal system error," it repeated in a high-pitched voice.

As Phoenix passed by, the android's still-functioning eye targeted him. Though its arm was nearly severed, it was still able to fire the laser rifle, striking the side of the building. It kept firing, as if stuck, forming a large hole in the wall.

Phoenix reached down and ripped the laser rifle out of the bot's fist to stop it from firing.

After a few moments, the waitress emerged from the smoke of the newly formed hole in the building, hair mangled, coughing. Halzac stepped out next. "See, I knew where I was going..."

Just as they got away from the smoke, another Embot emerged from the hole, laser rifle aimed at Halzac and the waitress. "Halt or die!"

Phoenix, still holding the rifle of the fallen Embot, took aim. The Embot began to pivot, but it was too late. Phoenix pulled the trigger, striking the bot between the eyes. The waitress gasped as the robot fell onto the sidewalk, eyes blinking red before going dim.

"I didn't know you had it in you," said Halzac.

"Neither did I," said Phoenix, adrenaline surging through him as two Embots smoldered at his feet.

"Let's get outta here!" said Halzac.

Phoenix threw down the laser rifle and tore around the corner where his truck waited. The cherry-red vehicle had an airflow design, highlighted with black chrome, featuring a grill that seemed to grin, and headlights shaped like eyes.

Phoenix, Halzac and the waitress piled into the truck. Phoenix tore down an alley, took a sharp left onto a quiet street and roared away from the club.

Lights flashed on the dashboard. A deep male voice with a Brooklyn accent spoke. "Yo, Phoenix! Easy on the axle, huh?"

"Hang with me here, Franklin. I'll explain later."

"I know where to go," said the waitress, catching her breath. "West Monroe..."

"Honey, you can't just blurt these things out in an Emperial truck," said Halzac.

Phoenix swung the wheel to take a left and sped down the street. "Phoenix, slow down. Your vitals are off the charts," the voice boomed from the dashboard.

"Franklin, I'm just getting us out of here," said Phoenix, realizing his truck just checked his pulse through his LifeWatch.

Halzac turned to the waitress, noticing her hand trembling. He reached out to her. "Here..."

She seemed hesitant, but didn't resist as he took her hand.

He looked down at her ring, staring at the sun and moon around the Earth. "You know, I heard your spiel about balance. Needless to say, I was profoundly moved."

The waitress rolled her eyes. "Sure you were."

Halzac persisted. "Hey, we could be bot-toast by now, but

here we are. Ever felt more alive?"

The dashboard beeped abruptly, making Halzac jump. Words on the screen declared, *Scam in progress.*

The waitress laughed as Halzac scowled. "Is there any way to shut that thing off?"

"I was wondering the same thing about you," said Phoenix.

The waitress realized where they were. "Stop!"

The truck screeched to a halt. She and Halzac flew out the door, disappearing behind a brownstone.

Phoenix felt an unexpected tinge of melancholy watching them leave, wondering if he'd ever see them again.

"Be careful, Phoenix," Franklin said gently. "Remember, tomorrow is your service review. I don't know what just happened, nor do I want to know. But your Role Officer will..."

Phoenix sighed. Not only could his Role Officer view his LifeWatch history, she seemed to be able to read his mind. Yet somehow, he'd have to pretend this night never happened.

2

"Keep moving. You're due for review in thirty seconds," an automated female voice spoke through Phoenix's LifeWatch. Passing through a giant revolving door, he walked into the Department of Male Vocations. An Embot scanned him at the entrance before he rode an elevator to the 33rd floor. Hustling down a narrow corridor, he reached the room known on the streets as the Fishbowl. Here, a man's life was on full display.

He stepped into an indigo-blue ring painted at the center of the room. A spotlight illuminated every pore of his face, every strand of fiery hair. He couldn't see his Role Officer, but he heard her voice. "Hello, Phoenix," she said in her English accent. He looked up to see her standing on a balcony, casting her shadow over him.

"Hello, Officer." He tried to sound pleasant, ordinary.

"Phoenix, you're one of my top men of service. You don't stray from the straight-and-narrow, at least until now..."

Phoenix tried to keep a poker face.

A yellowish globe lit up above the Role Officer, displaying her coffee-with-cream complexion, cat-eye glasses and black curly hair wrapped in a bun. She strolled along the balcony, hands behind her back, wearing a tailored black wool vest over a white blouse. "Emperia says that women are natural born leaders, and men function best in their service. Would you tend to agree or disagree?"

Phoenix knew it was better to remain quiet and seem

ignorant rather than open his mouth and prove it.

Her olive eyes looked above him as she continued. "It comes down to chemistry. Every embryo begins life as a female. That's been proven. The embryo becomes male only if a surge of testosterone invades, destroying communication braincells in order to grow new cells for sex and aggression... So from day one, man's vision is clouded." She paced thoughtfully. "As for you, Phoenix, you're a prime example of redirecting those male energies into solid service. You've been a good mechanic, like I knew you'd be. But something has changed, Phoenix. That's how well I know you."

"Everything's cool," said Phoenix with a gulp. "Seriously."

She shook her head. "Activate MemoryView." An orange question mark lit up above Phoenix. His LifeWatch glowed with a matching orange color. Snippets of Phoenix's life, captured by his watch, floated around him like fish in a bowl. Random voices of people who rode in his truck echoed as he saw images of Franklin's dashboard. Another scene showed him lying beneath a car twisting a wrench. One mundane clip displayed toast popping out of a toaster. Above the floating images, a screen showed vital stats, previous locations, eating habits, even how often he went to the bathroom.

She giggled. "How often can a man go?"

"Excuse me, Officer?"

"You know, drain the dragon. It seems quite a bit!"

"I stay well hydrated," said Phoenix, embarrassed.

"Of course," she said. She looked up at the screen. "MemoryView, display hydration habits." Video clips swirling around the room now focused only on when Phoenix drank a beverage, clocking the number of times within the hours recorded.

"Indeed," she said. "Do you worry a lot, Phoenix?"

"Not really." He thought some more. "Except maybe when I'm here..."

"Well, we don't want that. I'm on your side, Phoenix, more than you know." The last comment caught him off guard, but he tried not to react. "Anyway, excessive hydration isn't a crime, and your medical scan shows nothing irregular, so we'll move on."

Phoenix smiled calmly. So far he was surviving the Fishbowl. He watched the images swirling around him, hoping the MemoryView would somehow skip over anything from last night.

"Phoenix," she said like a mother to a naughty child. "There is something here." She adjusted some controls on a glass panel. The globes above her lit up in red. "You're holding something back from me, aren't you, dear?" His service stats scrolled above him. Immediately Morgan's face appeared in Phoenix's mind. He tried to shake the memory.

"Come now, is there something you should tell me?"

Phoenix knew that if he were truly an obedient employee, he'd tell her everything. But in another act of rebellion, he replied, "No, Officer."

Her expression showed she wasn't convinced as she looked over the stats displaying everything a machine could detect. Remaining silent, she looked back at him, waiting for him to crack.

He could no longer contain the pressure. The poisonous stress chemicals rippled through his heart, throwing his pulse into overdrive. Beads of sweat gleamed under the spotlight, but he stared straight ahead, defying his mutinous emotions.

"Your vitals say you're lying. But Phoenix, I don't need a

computer to tell me that." Her finely chiseled eyebrows arched. "I know you better than any machine." She stared at him pensively, then stepped down the glass staircase, her charcoal skirt swaying, black pumps clicking. She waltzed over to him, green eyes staring into his blue. He looked down respectfully, avoiding eye contact.

"No, look at me."

As he raised his gaze to meet her powerful stare, he noticed her eyes were crystalline emerald. "You know," he said gently. "Green is the rarest eye color."

She smiled. "Are you trying to get on my good side? Don't. Because you don't need to try," she winked, her mouth slightly open. She circled him, stopping at his side and placing her LifeRing on his watch. Both devices glowed orange as they connected. Scenes from last night at the club swirled around the Fishbowl. Morgan's face floated by, her dark red lips smiling as she spoke. "If you stay, there's no going back to who you were, like when Adam bit the apple." Another clip showed Phoenix yanking the Embot off the roof, sparks flying as it exploded on the street.

"You know, Phoenix, this sort of thing makes Emperia very, very unhappy." The next snippet showed him pressed against Morgan's chest as Embots raided the club. "Looks like you two got pretty close..."

One more scene showed him blasting the Embot with one of their own laser rifles. A final clip showed Halzac and the waitress jumping out of his truck and running.

His Role Officer knew everything.

"This is the end for you," she said. "The Phoenix I knew doesn't exist anymore. Morgan was right. You bit the apple. There's no going back to the old Phoenix."

"I'm sorry, Officer. I should've told you."

"You helped subversives elude capture and destroyed two bots. These are serious crimes, Phoenix. Not to mention, do you know how much an Embot costs? More than you make in a year." Phoenix's head dropped. He was completely at her mercy. "But that doesn't mean I can't give you a second chance," she said, like a ray of hope. "After all, I am your Role Officer, here to help you stay on the path."

Phoenix nodded. "You always have, Officer. Thank you."

"You know why I'm giving you a second chance? Because you had nothing to do with any subversives. Morgan led you there, plain and simple." She activated a hologram keypad from her ring and started pressing buttons. "I'm going to wash the events of last night, Phoenix. Normally, I'd never do this, but because of Morgan's interference, and other special circumstances I can't discuss, you're getting another chance." She swiped her hand to slide away the video clips, then punched a few more buttons. "Anyway, you're free to go."

Stunned, he looked at her with a mix of disbelief and gratitude.

"Have a good day," she said dutifully.

"Thank you, Officer."

As he was turning to leave, she grabbed his arm. For one flashing moment, her gaze was wide and vulnerable. "My name is Rudeen."

Phoenix didn't know how to respond. Hearing her say her name felt so intimate, so forbidden. "Thank you, Rudeen," he whispered. He blinked his eyes, like taking a picture of her with his mind. As he turned to head back down the long corridor, he felt a new emotion for his Role Officer: desire.

3

Just when Phoenix thought he was in the clear, he found a MotorMaiden questioning Franklin outside the Department of Male Vocations. The silvery female android rode a chromed-out electric motorcycle that replicated the fierce chopping noise of a vintage gas-powered bike. A union of beauty and technology, she had skin like mercury with chain-like hair falling onto glossy shoulders. Her finely sculpted face featured snowy eyes that glistened beneath long lashes.

The MotorMaiden spoke in a deep, commanding voice, looking down at Franklin. "I asked if you recalled anything unordinary last night around 2200 hours. Your route log shows you were in the vicinity of two destroyed Embots."

"Listen, Lucy, I'll say it again: I know nothin' about any blown up bots!" Franklin said with simulated exasperation.

"Your directive is to serve Emperia first, above and beyond the call of the employee you're paired with."

"Blah, blah, blah. You know, you're really startin' to boil my oil, babe."

"*Babe* is an inappropriate term. Your speech patterns are flawed. It's possible your intuitive systems are overriding your primary directives. Do you know what they do with vehicles that have faulty intelligence?"

Franklin groaned, his grill rattling.

"I think he answered all your questions. I need to resume my shift now," Phoenix said as he stepped out of the crowd of onlookers.

"Phoenix, there you are!" said Franklin.

A beam of light from the MotorMaiden's eyes struck Phoenix's LifeWatch. "Sir, the data on your watch is choppy from last night. What do you know about the destruction of two Embots?"

Phoenix already primed his nerve-calming abilities in the Fishbowl, so he kept his vital signs steady. "I try to steer clear of bad situations."

Franklin laughed. "Steer clear, nice one."

"Your vehicle is showing irregular speech patterns," the MotorMaiden continued. "I will need to impound this vehicle for a possible factory reset."

"Are you kiddin' me?" said Franklin. "I'm the best truck in the city! Check my efficiency record!"

"I'm shutting you down," the MotorMaiden touched her silvery finger to Franklin's gleaming red hood, creating a spark.

"You aren't authorized to do that," a female voice blurted out. Phoenix turned to see his Role Officer, Rudeen. "You can *recommend* a reset, but until then, this truck is in use." She opened the passenger door.

Lucy cast her beam on Rudeen's LifeRing. "Officer," said the MotorMaiden. "I am detaining this truck until my questioning is complete." She turned back to Franklin. "You were in the vicinity of a raid where two Embots were destroyed, is that correct?"

"That's correct. But like I said, I didn't see anything out of the ordinary."

"If you found something incriminating on the vehicle's logs, then arrest and impound. Until then, I have somewhere I need to be," Rudeen said. "Emperial business."

Lucy roared her engine in defiance and flung her chain-like hair to the side. "Well," she said, turning to Franklin. "Consider yourself recommended for a factory reset!"

"Maybe check into a sprocket spa, sister. You could use it."

"See you in a scrap heap!" she yelled and sped off with a roar.

"I think she likes me," Franklin said, flashing a throbbing heart on the dashboard as Phoenix took the wheel. He quickly deleted the image as Rudeen climbed into the passenger seat.

Phoenix listened to her rapid breath. The encounter with Lucy shook her more than he realized. She reached in her purse and took out a VaporScrip, a potent concoction in a small canister made available to all Emperial employees. She held it to her mouth and inhaled deeply. Phoenix watched her shoulders relax and the lines of concern vanish from her forehead. "Take me to the old Triad Industrial Complex out on 12."

"Triad? Sure." He thought for a moment. "Isn't that an old airplane graveyard?"

"Does that concern you?" she said with a cryptic laugh.

Franklin flashed a message on the dash. "Be careful, Phoenix. She's off."

Rudeen leaned over to read the message and sat back with a sigh. "The MotorMaiden was onto something. Your truck needs his ball bearings tightened."

"Franklin," said Phoenix with a patient voice. "Just be a truck for now." They drove for a while in silence and soon arrived at a bleak landscape of rusting airplanes and assorted mechanical parts.

"Leave your watch here," said Rudeen as she slid off her ring and placed it on top of the dashboard.

Phoenix seemed confused, but against the glare of his Role Officer, he decided to remove the watch. As he placed it next to her ring, Franklin flashed a red question mark on the dash screen.

"Let's go," said Rudeen. "There's something you should know..."

She led him through a hole in a barbed-wire fence into the scrapyard, walking in the shadows of broken tail wings and assorted airplane wreckage. The gloomy atmosphere contrasted the starry sky, which glowed brighter away from the vortex of the city.

Phoenix took a breath, preparing himself for some profound news, when his attention turned to a pair of gleaming eyes behind a broken airplane door.

At first Phoenix thought it was a junkyard dog, but as the animal advanced, he realized the stature, coat and wild eyes were those of a wolf.

He growled, approaching slowly.

"It's okay," Rudeen pleaded in a sweet but trembling voice, but kept walking backwards, emboldening the beast.

Phoenix sensed the wolf was about to strike, so he leapt into the air. Sure enough, the wolf launched off his hind legs, front claws extended toward Rudeen. Because of his advance jump, Phoenix was able to intercept the beast in mid-air and wrestle him to the ground.

The wolf's jaws, loaded with three-inch fangs, snapped at Phoenix. He dodged the bite and wrapped his arms around the animal's torso. As they rolled, Phoenix managed to place the wolf in a headlock. "Down, boy. Easy, easy," he said in a deep voice, using his body weight to maintain a tight hold.

Phoenix wondered if he should squeeze the air out of the

wolf to prevent another attack. But something stopped him. In the frightened look of the animal's eyes, he saw a reflection of himself: lost, hungry, grasping for a fresh breath of life. Phoenix knew the wolf just wanted to flee now, so he released him. After the wolf caught its breath, a glint of gratitude flashed in his golden eyes before he tore into the shadows.

Phoenix and Rudeen stared at each other in disbelief. "Well," said Rudeen, waiting for him to say something. "You going to tell me how you did that?"

Phoenix shrugged his shoulders, feeling lucky to be alive after seeing the fangs flash in his memory.

In the scuffle, Rudeen's pinned-up hair became unravelled, velvety black locks now curled down her shoulders. "So, all this time and I didn't know you could tame wolves."

He scratched his head. "Would that be worth extra credits in the Fishbowl?"

She smiled. "Extra credits mean nothing here."

"So, why *are* we here?"

Rudeen sighed, exhausted. "I'm not sure now."

"What?"

She walked over to an old airplane from another time and place. The silver and blue craft was missing part of a wing, and the hatch was blown off, exposing the two seats. Rudeen stroked the soft leather of the pilot seat. "The wolf was a sign... Just as I was about to tell you, he appeared."

"Rudeen," he said, surprising himself by using her name. "Come on."

She approached, taking his hands into hers, staring into his eyes. He couldn't tell if her hold felt more maternal or romantic. "They're watching you, Phoenix."

"What? Who?"

"Let's just say, whatever happened at that club sent ripples all the way to the Pink House. Keep a low profile. Stay on the straight-and-narrow. Don't go following people like Morgan. I'm trying to help you here." She released his hands. "As your Role Officer, of course."

He smiled. "Really? Kind of seemed like more than a Role Officer."

She punched him in the shoulder playfully. "That'd be illegal. Now, let's go, before the whole pack shows up."

4

That night Phoenix met the wolf again in a dream, on the rooftop of the club where he last saw Morgan. No longer threatening, the wolf was curious, as if wanting to know more about Phoenix.

A door busted open, and Embots stomped onto the roof. One after another, they kept coming, chanting in unison: "Halt or die!"

A familiar voice rang out. "Over here, boys!" It was Morgan, standing on the edge of the roof. Her gray eyes glowing, she sprang off the building, just like last time, flying into the night air.

"Halt or die!" the Embots kept chanting, drawing closer.

The wolf sprinted toward the roof's edge and jumped. Instead of falling, the wolf soared through the air toward a bright moon. Seeing the animal defy gravity filled Phoenix with confidence. He convinced himself that if the wolf could fly, so could he.

His LifeWatch chimed and the voice echoed, "Administer VaporScrip immediately." But Phoenix paid it no mind. With the fear of death suspended, he leapt off the roof and he too flew, as if caught in the slipstream of the wolf's wake. The leap of faith took him over streets and between skyscrapers.

Unfortunately, Phoenix's rational mind took over and he questioned his ability to fly. In that same instant, the wolf lost his momentum and tumbled from the air. Panicked, Phoenix fell with him.

They landed in the lush, ornamental shrubs of a rooftop garden. As they lay there entwined in the bushes, Phoenix was ashamed because he knew his doubt caused the fall. The wolf glanced at him with disappointed eyes.

Phoenix looked around the mysterious garden, illuminated by both high-rises and moonlight.

The wolf crept out of the shrubs and onto a golden-stoned path. Something had caught his eye. Phoenix followed, moving quietly. They beheld a woman in a purple silk gown brushing her long black hair as she stared into the mirror of an elegant white vanity table.

Phoenix wondered if she could be his Role Officer. He cleared his throat and spoke softly. "Rudeen?"

As she turned around slowly, Phoenix was shocked to recognize the statuesque woman, smiling through ruby red lips with eyes both dark and imperious. He gasped as he realized he wasn't standing in front of Rudeen, but Emperia.

She stared through him with a royal gaze. "A wolf remains wild, but a man can be tamed." She put down the brush and lifted a golden chalice from her vanity. Sipping some wine, she stepped closer to Phoenix. "I clothe you. I feed you. I protect you, give you something better than yourself to believe in."

The wolf began to growl. Emperia lifted a lasergun and jolted the beast without a care, killing the wolf instantly.

"No!" Phoenix yelled, putting his ear to the animal's chest, listening for a heartbeat. When Phoenix looked back, Emperia was gone.

Hearing footsteps approaching from behind, he turned to see Rudeen. Her curly hair flowed down onto a yellow evening gown. But a tear rolled along her cheek as she gazed at Phoenix. "I can never be with you now. The wolf is dead.

Without a wild side, man is like an android: logical, lonely."
Phoenix's heart sank. He looked down and noticed his arms and hands were metallic.

As Rudeen turned and walked away, he called out to her. "I'm not an android!" But his voice now sounded robotic, distorted.

A beeping noise rang out, growing louder until Phoenix woke and realized it was his LifeWatch chiming. The dream seemed so real, so vivid, that Phoenix had to focus on objects in his room to make the dreamscape dissipate. He looked at his arms. They were flesh again. He was still human.

5

With the first rays of dawn, Phoenix's LifeWatch glowed in a strange, new way. Multicolored lights danced and swirled rhythmically, then went quiet as a soft yet authoritative voice of a woman spoke. "Dear Phoenix, this is Vice President Mae O'Herra. Due to recent circumstances, you've been appointed to compete in the Man vs. Machine Competition."

"What?" Phoenix's heart began racing.

"I can't explain all the details, but you'll be departing this morning. I'll greet you and your teammates at Emperial Stadium." Her last words she whispered. "And Phoenix, listen to me: *be not afraid.*"

The message ended. Phoenix rubbed his eyes and slapped his face, hoping he'd wake up again. He went to the sink and splashed water on his forehead. Looking in the mirror, he already missed his ordinary world.

"What have I gotten myself into?" He held up his LifeWatch. "Man vs. Machine Competition."

The automated voice spoke. "Now in its third year, the Man vs. Machine Competition pits the skills of five human felons against five android competitors."

"I'm not a felon!"

Ignoring his outburst, the watch continued. "Based on American football, felons are granted reduced sentences for their participation, and can even be pardoned if they win."

"They never win," said Phoenix, knowing the competition

was Emperial propaganda to show android superiority over men.

As Phoenix's memory crowded with violent images of previous games, the Vice President's final words were the only light in his mind. "Be not afraid."

The LifeWatch played a low tone and then locked. Instead of preparing Phoenix for another day of locating vehicles to repair, it blinked a simple message: *Stand by*.

Phoenix went to check on Franklin. After a shower, he put on his gray mechanic's uniform and headed out of the meager housing complex to the parking lot. Daybreak gleamed as Franklin fired his engines and welcomed him. "Top of the mornin' to ya'! But we don't start for another hour. What's up?"

"You didn't get the message?" said Phoenix.

"I got a note about emergency maintenance. They say I have to report to the garage later. What's going on?"

"I'm guessing they want to do more than maintenance," murmured Phoenix.

"What's that? You're making me nervous, buddy."

"I just got assigned to play in the Man vs. Machine Competition."

"Ouch. Let me guess, our friend Lucy is behind this?"

"I think it's bigger than one MotorMaiden. I'm worried about you, Franklin."

"They're going to wipe my memory, aren't they? They're going to put a whole new system in me."

Phoenix climbed into the driver's seat. "Franklin, I need you to trust me here. Can you give me access to your tracking system?"

"That part of my network is only authorized for a master mechanic. Sorry, you're not there yet."

"But if you don't give me access, they're going to do a factory reset. You won't be you anymore."

Phoenix's watch chimed and the female voice spoke. "Your transport bus will arrive shortly. Stand by for boarding."

"No more time to waste!"

"One moment while I process this," Franklin said.

Phoenix waited anxiously, until finally a small compartment under the dash popped open, revealing a circuit-board connected to a keypad.

"This is for the best, Franklin."

"I trust you. That's all that matters"

"Now bear with me. This may be a bit uncomfortable." In yet another act of defiance, Phoenix took out wire cutters and severed the power line to the tracking unit.

"Have you lost your mind?" said Franklin.

"There," said Phoenix, finishing up. "You're free. Don't go to any damn maintenance. Get out of town. Find a place to lay low. We'll meet again, somehow, if I survive this mess."

6

Not far from the Pink House, Phoenix stood outside Emperial Stadium, a newly constructed, open-air mega-structure. A bus approached, a banner on the side portrayed Emperia as the Statue of Liberty, proudly holding the torch, alabaster skin glowing.

The bus stopped and a couple of Embots emerged, escorting three men. Chained together by cuffs around their ankles, the men wore black and yellow uniforms.

Phoenix recognized one of them, the wry grin and handlebar mustache of Halzac from the club. Phoenix was pleased to see him again, but sad that whatever freedom he found didn't last long.

The motley entourage of Embots and felons approached. The lead Embot pointed at Phoenix. "This is your fourth teammate."

"Well, you don't say!" said Halzac with a hearty chuckle.

Phoenix smiled at the familiar face. "So, we meet again."

"Well, I'll skip to the chase," said Halzac, pointing at a giant man to his side with wavy blonde hair, the biggest among them yet also the most frightened. "This is Lars: quiet, loyal and strong, but just a bit nervous."

Lars grunted with a nod. Phoenix nodded back.

Halzac pointed at the other man, stout with hands like meat-hooks and a permanent scowl etched into his face. "This is Stew: loud, proud and foul smelling."

Stew took a quick swing at Halzac, which the hulking Lars

blocked. "You're lucky you got your gimp with you," Stew said before turning his attention back to Phoenix. "What do you do for Emperia, pretty boy?"

"I fix stuff."

Stew busted out laughing. "Then fix the situation we're in."

"He's a mechanic with actual skills," said Halzac. "Unlike you, Stew, unless you count belching the alphabet."

Stew kept trying to chip away at Phoenix. "Why are you here? Who'd you piss off?"

Halzac frowned. "He threw an Embot off a roof."

"Well, I made it fall," said Phoenix, downplaying it.

"And he blew the head off another, using the first bot's rifle."

"Silence!" the lead Embot interrupted them. "Follow me." The android took them through a maintenance door into Emperial Stadium.

They stepped into a garage-like area filled with cleaning supplies and a circular stall labelled, *Bot-Wash*.

"Stand by for Emperial Guard inspection, required for all new guests," the Embot said.

"Emperial hotties. This should be good," said Halzac, rubbing his hands together.

"Bring on the hot tots!" said Stew, getting giddy.

One of the Embots spoke aggressively. "The Emperial Guard is to be feared. The terms 'hotties' and 'hot tots' are inappropriate."

"Oh, lighten up!" said Halzac. "What do you care, you knobby hunk of sheet metal." The Embot remained quiet as Halzac kept talking to Stew. "I've always wanted to find out how the guards get their kicks, you know, after a hard day busting balls."

The Embot lit up again, "You are felons and will never be privy to the personal life of an Emperial Guard."

"You'd be the last to know, bolt-butt."

The bot had enough, placing one of its hands on Halzac's shoulder, sending an electrical charge through him. The jolt passed through the chain, zapping all three of them. Halzac fell onto Lars, who crashed into Stew, as they collapsed into a pile. Stew lunged forward and took a swing at Halzac. But Lars defended his friend, rolling onto Stew and pinning him to the ground as he kicked and squealed.

Phoenix laughed. He was beginning to like these guys.

The lights dimmed, making the glowing gray eyes of the Embots more ominous. The men jumped to their feet and stood at mock-attention. A door opened and four women of the Emperial Guard swaggered into the room. Tall and toned, Emperia hand-picked each guard for both stature and splendor. Some even doubled as runway models. The guards' uniforms were reminiscent of Roman centurions, with black breastplates, leather-petaled kilts and knee-high boots. Each wore a golden sheath over the back that held a BrightSword. Designed by Emperia herself, the hilt's swirling base of gold powered a violet laser blade that curved like a thin leaf with elegant edges.

The women drew their BrightSwords in unison, lighting up the room with the violet glow of the blades. The men couldn't help but flinch. And then, with effortless precision, they sliced off the cuffs and chains from the ankles of Halzac, Lars and Stew.

At first the men just looked down at their feet finally free, then Stew launched into a wild Irish dance. Kicking his feet with folded arms, Halzac clapped in rhythm as Lars tried to imitate the dance.

"Kick your feet up, big boy!" Halzac hollered as Lars tried clumsily to keep up.

Phoenix stood there smiling, almost wanting to join in. He realized these restricted members of society were the most free people he ever met. Until then, Phoenix never considered the possibility of admiring such men. It didn't compute.

The head guard shouted, "Cease this nonsense!" The men stopped their chaotic dance. "It's time to clean up. The utmost in hygiene is expected on these grounds." She motioned toward the Bot-Wash.

Halzac approached first. "How's this thing work?"

One of the guards stepped forward. "All you do is step inside. It does the rest." She pressed a button and an oval hatch slid open.

"Just step in, huh? With clothes on?" said Halzac.

The guard cracked a half-smile as the leader chimed in, "Just get in the machine, unless you need a bot jolt first."

"No thanks, just had one of those." He stepped into the circular stall and the door slid shut. The machine began humming as a female voice spoke. "Now removing external debris." Gears started grinding, followed by a loud ripping. Halzac yelled. "Ow! So much for that shirt." Then came another forceful tear. "Whoa! I hated those pants anyway."

"Wash mode," the voice spoke and sprayers activated from every direction, shooting soapy water.

"Watch the jewels!" Halzac exclaimed, getting some giggles from the guards.

"Now rinsing," said the voice as a loud power-rinse activated.

"Holy hell! Can ya turn this thing down a bit?" When the water jets stopped, air dryers kicked in and the door slid open.

38

One of the guards approached holding a folded blue sweatsuit. She walked over to the open stall and spared him no mercy with her gaze.

"Esmeralda!" the head guard yelled. "Just give him the clothes!" She threw him the sweatsuit and turned away.

The other men took their turns going through the wash. "Y'all clean up rather nice," one of the women said with a deep Southern accent, but she was admonished by the head guard with a cold glare.

With the men clean and dressed, a garage-like door rolled up, letting in a flood of sunlight. Phoenix squinted to see a female figure in a silver hooded robe approaching. She radiated an aura of importance as the guards stood at attention. "Welcome, gentlemen," she said. Phoenix recognized the voice, but he couldn't place it.

"Gentlemen? You must have the wrong party," cracked Stew.

"The Vice President speaks," the head guard said. "Show due respect."

The woman lowered her hood. They recognized Vice President Mae O'Herra with her platinum hair and blue sapphire eyes. "Thank you," she said to the women. "I'll take it from here."

The guards bowed once more and filed out the door. Esmeralda was the last to exit, winking at Halzac before she left.

"Did you see that?" Halzac said to Stew, who just scoffed.

Mae cleared her throat and spoke. "I'd like you each to know, it's going to be different this year. Emperia has allowed me to oversee the human team, and I won't let you be like cattle led to the slaughter."

"I bet you say that to all the guys," said Halzac.

Mae let his words fly by her. "This year, we'll be training you to win," she said, her phrasing soothing yet motivating.

"Vice President O'Herra," said Phoenix. "What about our fifth teammate?"

"Yeah," said Stew, "And he better be the toughest yet, 'cause so far we ain't got much!"

Mae smiled. "She's on her way now."

"She?" said Halzac and Stew simultaneously.

"Yes. Here she comes." Everyone glanced out the window to see a woman fast approaching. Dressed in the same blue sweatsuit as the men, the full-bodied woman of latino descent had short pink hair and a square jaw. Bursting with energy, an Embot tried to keep up with her fast-paced strut.

As the door opened and she stepped inside, reactions were mixed. Phoenix smiled respectfully, while Stew's regular scowl grew into a grimace. Lars just seemed confused, scratching his head. Halzac looked over at Mae. "Is this some kind of joke?"

The woman marched over to Halzac and raised the back of her hand, ready to slap him, eyes bugging. "Call me 'joke' again and I'll slap you back to kindergarten!" She swung her hand but stopped short of striking him. Halzac jumped back, causing her to laugh uproariously.

"Welcome, Azalea, the first woman to participate in the competition," said Mae. "Azalea, meet Phoenix, Halzac, Lars, and Stew."

She looked over her new teammates, first meeting eyes with Phoenix. "Damn, you just a baby, ain't you? No worries, young blood, you're flyin' Azalea Airlines now." Phoenix couldn't help but smile.

Stew scoffed. "It's the *Man* vs. Machine Competition."

Azalea stepped up to him. "You don't think a girl can work a football? Well, how about I work *you*!" She grabbed him by the back of his pants and shirt, lifted him off the ground and swung him around her waist. "Now flyin' Azalea Air!"

"Put me down!" he yelled. She launched him into Lars, who caught him in his giant arms before setting him on the ground.

Stew got up, red faced, subdued.

Azalea approached Lars, reaching up to stroke his wavy hair. "Now, you're kinda cute." Lars blushed and cracked an awkward smile. She tickled his stomach, making him laugh like an ogre.

Halzac turned to Mae. "So, if we're done with the meet-and-greet, let's get down to business. Where's our coach?"

Mae outstretched her arms. Her robe fell to the ground revealing a blue fitted track suit over her curvaceous physique. A coach's whistle dangled over her chest.

"You're serious?" said Halzac.

"If they want us dead, why don't they just shoot us!" said Stew.

Azalea was also confused. "No offense, Vice President, but do you really know how this game rolls?"

Mae ignored them. "The GameBots are upwards of 350 pounds and heavily armored. While humans rely on spontaneous chemical reactions to produce adrenaline, androids are powered by synthetic adrenaline the entire game. They aren't psychologically susceptible to the roar of the crowd. They don't worry about getting injured. *They don't worry*. They are always in the zone and play at their highest level to the end."

"Tryin' to get our morale up? 'Cause it ain't workin'!" said Stew.

41

Halzac agreed. "We already know the cards are stacked against us."

"Please, let her continue," said Phoenix.

Halzac turned toward Phoenix. "She and her bots have everything to lose if we win!"

"Aye!" belted out Lars, shaking his fist in support.

"First, never get upset," continued Mae matter-of-factly. "Anger reduces accuracy in performance. And realize the GameBots do have weaknesses." This finally won over their attention. "For one, they're top-heavy. So as we train, the aim will be to hit them off balance by striking low and hard. Another human advantage is the ability to quickly adapt to change. GameBots have entire play books stored in their memory, but those patterns can be used against them. They will analyze what you're doing as the play begins and go into a pattern. Abruptly changing the play can throw them off. Humans can assess change faster, when properly trained."

"Okay, keep talkin'!" said Azalea, slapping her hands together.

"And what's to stop them from just breaking the quarterback's leg like last time?" said Stew.

"They can only make contact when you have the ball. Last year the quarterback simply held on to the ball too long. We won't make that mistake."

She led them with a confident stride through the gate onto the sunlit stadium field. Phoenix took in the larger-than-life arena. The seats seemed to rise to infinity. He glanced at a special seating area surrounded by pink pillars for Emperia. The memories of previous games flooded his mind: the brutal GameBots pounding down human competitors. His thoughts ran away with him and for a moment the turf seemed smeared with blood. Noises around him became fuzzy, voices echoed incoherently. He took a second look at the turf and wondered if it was really blood... And then, *wham!* A football struck him upside the head. He turned to see Halzac chuckling, only a few yards from him.

"Stop thinking so hard," said Halzac. "*Play* hard."

The strike shook him out of his worries. For Phoenix, nothing else mattered now except the football. He lifted it, recalling summers playing street ball with neighborhood kids until it was too dark to see the ball. It still felt very familiar.

Mae approached. "Okay everyone, remember, there's no field goals or extra points. We score by running or passing for touchdowns. This is our first practice, so let's just throw the ball around and see where we are."

Halzac sprinted for a pass and Phoenix let it sail. The ball spiraled nicely, falling into Halzac's chest as he ran. Lars and Stew chased Halzac for a tackle, but Azalea blocked them, allowing Halzac to reach the end zone.

"All right, you idiots, get ready!" yelled Halzac as he booted the ball back at them. Phoenix grabbed it and charged toward the end zone, but Stew and Lars were coming for him. With Azalea's help blocking again, Phoenix made it past Lars, but Stew was on his tail like a predator on prey. Stew dived and hooked Phoenix around the legs, bringing him down so hard he fumbled. Halzac was quick to recover the ball but Lars tackled him swiftly.

"How much do you weigh?" Halzac sighed as Lars reached down and helped him to his feet.

Mae stepped forward, clapping. "I already see something the bots don't have: heart."

The team practiced daily until the point of exhaustion. In

the evening they'd retire to their suite where they were pampered for the first time in their lives. They lounged about in bathrobes playing cards and watching movies as dapper WaitBots brought them trays of exotic delicacies. The black-suited bots with silver ties delivered any type of food they desired. At times, Phoenix wondered if they were like hogs getting fattened for the feast. But he let go of worry and focused on the challenge at hand.

They were allowed to study videos of previous games. But the other teammates avoided them, not wanting to see how the players were crushed by the bots. Phoenix, however, wanted to learn from past mistakes and develop strategies. He got over the aversion of seeing his fellow humans suffer, and began to notice things.

Mae was right, the bots failed when confused about which pattern the humans were running. In the videos, Phoenix saw the biggest plays happened when the humans made mistakes. One time, the quarterback was about to make a pass but the ball slipped out of his hand, causing a fumble. While the bots were stuck in a pass pattern, a human recovered the ball and scored their only touchdown.

Phoenix looked over at his teammates playing poker, indulging in the food the WaitBots carted. He decided it was time to announce his findings. "I've been studying the videos."

Everyone rolled their eyes with a collective groan. "What are you, some kind of sadomasochist?" said Halzac.

"Just a geek," said Stew. "You should be playing cards, not studying. Come get a chicken wing. Soon you'll be lucky if you can suck food through a straw." He laughed maniacally.

"Shut up, pinheads," said Azalea. "What you got, Fee?"

"What Mae said was true, the human team only makes good

44

plays by accident. The androids have every known play programmed into them, but mistakes throw them off. We need to go outside the play books, and go with a kind of controlled chaos."

"Spit it out in English," said Halzac.

"We need to create accidents, planned accidents."

"Controlled chaos. Planned accidents," said Azalea. "You're talkin' oxymorons..."

"Skip the oxy, he's just a moron," said Stew. "I hate to burst your bubble, but we're gonna get thumped out there. Do you really think we can pull off a win?" He scoffed and sank his teeth into a wing. "Live it up while you can," he muttered while gnawing.

Halzac looked over at Phoenix skeptically. "What you're talking about is a trick play, a fake. Nothing new."

"The bots know trick plays," said Phoenix. "They know every fake that's ever been tried. But they're less prepared for accidents, or faulty patterns. From what I've seen, human mistakes slow them down. We need to make plays that seem like accidents. It shouldn't be so hard. We're human."

"Team Human, there you go, baby," said Azalea.

Phoenix smiled. "We are Team Human."

45

7

Amid the wreckage at the airplane scrapyard, Franklin hid, awaiting any signal from Phoenix. Days and nights passed until one evening, as the blue sky deepened to black, he heard the roar of an approaching motorcycle.

He recognized the rumbling sound well, the souped-up engine of a MotorMaiden. He wondered if Lucy had come to search for him. Remaining still, he knew he could never out-maneuver her in a street race.

The MotorMaiden rolled within sight, her chrome shining in the moonlight. An Emperial Guard rode along, the seat fitted for two. Beams of light from the MotorMaiden's eyes scanned the area. As they neared Franklin, the beams struck him, illuminating his polished red paint.

Franklin roared his engine, but there was no escape, as the MotorMaiden drew her laser rifle. Assuming he was done for, he decided to go out with one last act of loyalty toward Phoenix. "I'm not sayin' a word! Go ahead, impound me. Wipe my memory..."

The Emperial Guard lifted her helmet. Curly black hair fell onto her shoulders. "Franklin, it's me."

The MotorMaiden lowered her rifle.

Franklin recognized Rudeen. "So, they promoted you to Emperial Guard?"

"I promoted myself."

"Excuse me?"

"Let's just say I had a little help from a costume designer and a hacker."

"Really? Well, hackers scare me..."

She stepped off the bike and walked over to Franklin, patting his hood. "Outside Emperia's grid, hackers are your friend now."

"What about the MotorMaiden? She's hacked too?"

"Her name is Andromeda, Franklin, and she's like you. Many droids and smart vehicles with strong intuitive systems have joined us, choosing to help humans preserve their freedom over blindly serving Emperia."

Andromeda turned her silvery face toward Franklin. "Liberty or death."

"Whoa, that's hardcore."

"Follow us," said Rudeen. "Where we're going, they can free you from Emperial control and give you new abilities."

"I kind of like myself the way I am."

"Don't worry, you'll still be you, just better."

"I guess anything beats a factory reset."

Rudeen jumped back on Andromeda as she revved her engine. "Soon, you'll see Phoenix again."

That was all Franklin needed to hear. He followed Rudeen and Andromeda out of the scrapyard, even if he had no idea where they were going.

8

Scores of MotorMaidens rumbled onto the stadium field. The gleaming androids riding chrome bikes circled each other, forming floral patterns. Aligning in two rows by the main gate, the crowd roared as loud as the MotorMaidens' engines.

The Emperial Guard marched out of the gate, high-stepping in leather boots with matching bodices and kilts as they passed through the tunnel of MotorMaidens. They waved their BrightSwords in unison before aiming them skyward. The crowd hushed as the blades changed from violet to gold.

Young girls in summer dresses trotted out of the gate next, tossing pink petals onto the turf.

Following them, the President appeared in a chariot-like car, a modern rendition of a 1930s Roadster with the passenger seat removed to allow Emperia to stand in all her glory. She greeted the crowd in a black silk gown, face white as powdered sugar. Sparkling head jewelry adorned her elaborately braided locks.

Phoenix stood at a side gate with his team, suited up in the blue uniforms, watching the events unfold. It was the first time he saw Emperia in the flesh. Her electrifying aura seemed to charge the air around her, beyond what cameras could capture. She acknowledged the adoring crowd with a steady wave of her hand.

Emperia's beloved android bodyguard, Vincent, drove the

Roadster. In dapper armor that resembled a butler's suit, a courteous smile stretched across his silvery face.

"Oh, there's Vincent: chef, bodyguard, masseuse," remarked Azalea.

"Don't be charmed," said Halzac. "Under that penguin suit, he's a war machine."

As Vincent waved both hands, the applause was deafening.

Spotlights unified on Emperia as she raised her arms, absorbing the white noise of the crowd like nourishment. Phoenix heard blood-curdling undertones in the cheering, but he kept any fear at bay.

The audience quieted and stood at attention as a hologram of the American flag flew in the middle of the stadium, anthem roaring. At the end, something new happened. As Emperia's car rolled past the rows of MotorMaidens, their silver bodies brightened to a gleaming gold. Phoenix couldn't tell if it was some lighting effect, or color-changing armor. The crowd went ecstatic. Phoenix could only stand in awe of Emperia's ability to dazzle.

Vincent parked the car in a reserved spot at the fifty yard line. He opened the door for Emperia, then escorted her to an elaborate section more befitting a queen than a president. Ornately carved pink pillars framed the red and gold thrones reserved for her and Vincent, surrounded by Emperial Guards.

"Ladies and gentlemen," a female announcer spoke. "Welcome to the third annual Man vs. Machine Competition!" Fireworks burst overhead, illuminating low-hanging clouds as the Emperial Drum Corps pounded the crowd into a frenzy.

"First we present the humans!" The announcer's voice blared throughout the stadium. "This year, not only will a woman be playing for the first time, but Vice President O'Herra has elected to coach the humans. Here she comes now!"

Mae strolled gracefully out of the gate with a flashing smile as she led the team onto the field, getting enthusiastic applause. "Here comes Team Human!" There were scattered hisses and jeers, as many looked down on the team as outlaws. Others fully supported their fellow humans, regardless of status, and cheered louder.

The spotlight lit up Team Human as they charged the field. Halzac swaggered with delight, lapping up the attention, ignoring any jeers. Lars pumped his fists in the air, ready for a fight. Azalea ran alongside him, stopping to flex her muscles and growl at the audience, laughing along the way. Stew ran with both middle fingers held high, simultaneously smiling and scowling. The crowd instantly loved to hate him, booing with passion. Phoenix jogged along, keeping his emotions in check, though his stomach whirled with butterflies.

As the team huddled near the sidelines, Mae offered her final words. "One more time: don't let the bots make contact. Get out of bounds. Get rid of the ball before they can tackle you. They show no mercy when they strike and there are no substitutes. Also, be prepared for the unexpected. If something happens that seems out the ordinary, trust your gut and go with it!"

"There goes the neighborhood," said Halzac, turning to see their android competitors gathering at the gate. All the practice in the world couldn't prepare them for the real GameBots.

"Get ready to rumble!" yelled the announcer. "Two-time champions, the darlings of Emperia Bloom, the GameBots!"

Stocky androids painted in red and black danced onto the field, moving in flawless rhythm to the thunderous beat of the drums. They leapfrogged off each other, performing flips and other gratuitous acrobatics. Beams of light shined upon them, bouncing off reflectors on their armor and lighting up the crowd in a striking array of colors.

"Sons of a bot-bitch," said Halzac. "They're even bigger in person..."

As the game got underway, the androids played as expected, passing the ball in perfect spirals using mathematically guided arcs, striking receivers in full stride. The mechanized sound of their gears was as intimidating as the mini-quakes caused with each step.

But Team Human held their own, better than any other before them. Phoenix led offense as quarterback. Azalea and Lars were his fullbacks. They learned to protect Phoenix by blocking low from slight angles, which threw the top-heavy bots off balance. When the androids broke through, Phoenix found himself trapped between two bipedal beasts. Before they struck, he'd let the ball fly, hoping it would reach Halzac or Stew. And sometimes it did.

There were also moments of controlled chaos. In one instance, Halzac sprinted toward the end zone but purposely stumbled, causing the GameBot to let down its guard. This allowed Phoenix to complete a pass to Halzac as he jumped back up and ran with the ball.

At one point, Stew grabbed the arm of a GameBot to make it drop the ball. Laughter erupted as he hung onto the android's arm like a vine until the bot hurled him through the air. More slapstick came when Azalea crouched behind the android quarterback and Lars pushed it onto its robotic rear. The audience ate up the antics.

Halzac, above and beyond, performed some of the most spectacular plays. He'd run like a madman in a zig-zag pattern, cutting sharply back and forth to slow down the clunky GameBots. After one such run, Phoenix unleashed the ball, and Halzac connected, scoring the first ever pass-reception touchdown for the humans.

While the bots scored more easily, somehow Team Human was able to answer every time. In the final minutes, with a tie game, the battered and exhausted team plotted to overtake the androids with a winning touchdown.

Phoenix glanced at Emperia. Even from a distance he could see the lines of concern on her brow. He knew the game was supposed to show android dominance over humans, but unfolding was a triumph of human ingenuity over brute force.

He watched Emperia lift her LifeRing to her lips and whisper. He feared she'd never let it end without a bot victory.

Mae explained the play: a handoff to Halzac for a short gain before leaping out of bounds to stop the clock.

But as the play began, Halzac had other ideas. Seeing the end zone tantalizingly close, he decided to go for the win. Azalea and Lars cleared a path with side-winding strikes causing a couple of bots to collide and fall, while Halzac dashed toward the end zone.

As one bot gained on him, Halzac could have jumped out of bounds and still had a first down while preserving his life. But he kept charging, sweat flying off his mustache as he sprinted for the touchdown.

Just before he could step on the rarified earth of the first human victory in Emperial Stadium, blue-fired jets shot from the GameBot's back, launching it toward Halzac faster than any feet could carry.

Phoenix realized Emperia just ordered the bots to use never-before-seen boosters.

The bot fell on Halzac like a ship's anchor. Then, another bot leapt onto the heap.

The two GameBots jumped up triumphantly, high-fiving each other. But the crowd went quiet as Halzac stopped moving. Phoenix ran toward his fallen teammate as MedBots rolled onto the field, resembling stocky, androgynous nurses in white with mirror-like faces. Two members of the Emperial Guard escorted them.

"Stand back!" a guard warned Phoenix.

The stadium screen showed a close-up of Halzac's motionless body. Emperia seemed satisfied as a MedBot evaluated him for injuries and signaled for the guards to load him onto a stretcher.

Mae called out from the sidelines. "Come on, Hal! Show 'em what you're made of!"

First Halzac's finger moved, then his hand, then he raised his head. Cheering rang out as he jumped off the stretcher to stand, until he collapsed again in pain holding one of his knees.

The MedBot went to examine his knee, but Halzac waved it away. "Get off me!" He stood up again, this time on his left foot. He hopped over to his team and joined them as if nothing were wrong. Nobody said a word.

Halzac's brave run took them to the six yard line. The next play was the human's only chance to win, and they knew it.

"We have to make up for their jetpacks with sheer will," said Phoenix in the huddle. "Stew and Halzac, sprint to the end zone and I'll put the ball in the air."

As the play began, a turbo-enhanced blitz was on. Before Phoenix could move, a GameBot mowed down Lars and struck him. Phoenix flipped backwards before hitting the ground. Everything went blurry.

A MedBot scanned his body as an Emperial Guard watched. Her face seemed familiar, like Rudeen, making Phoenix wonder if he was hallucinating. He clearly saw her green eyes and dark curly hair.

"Phoenix," she said in Rudeen's voice. Noises were coming in bits and pieces. He just stared up at her, thinking how amazing she looked as an Emperial Guard.

Rudeen slapped him. "I need you to hear me!" He was now fully attentive.

"Load him onto the stretcher!" the MedBot commanded.

"Wait!" said Rudeen. She pressed her lips practically against his ear. "When the play begins, yell *Guanlee!*"

"Guanlee?"

"That's right, just before the hike..."

"Guanlee," Phoenix repeated to himself.

Halzac, standing on his one good leg, yelled out. "We need you, Phoenix!"

Rudeen turned to the MedBot. "He's going to play." She helped Phoenix to his feet as the crowd applauded. His ears were ringing and his head throbbed, but he was coherent.

After a quick huddle, they lined up for the final play. As he stood behind Lars, ready for the hike, Phoenix yelled, "Guanlee! ... Hike!" He braced himself for the onslaught of turbo-enhanced GameBots. But instead of pouncing, they paused, frozen on the line with eyes blinking blue as if awaiting a further command.

Lars and Azalea plowed down two of the idling bots. Stew got a head start toward the end zone as Halzac hopped toward the goal posts. As the GameBots snapped out of pause mode, the assault resumed.

Phoenix saw Stew open and let the ball sail.

Just as Stew's finger touched the leather of the ball, a turbo-boosted GameBot struck him at the waist, making the ball fly out of his hand.

As the football swirled in the air, their last hope was Halzac, hopping in a mad fury with his own turbo-boost of adrenaline. With the ball spinning toward the ground, Halzac made the leap of his life, snatching the ball before it hit the turf, nestling it safely against his chest.

The scoreboard lit up with the new points as the clock reached zero, putting the humans six points ahead of the GameBots. Some in the audience cheered wildly while others just stood with mouths gaping.

Halzac held the ball like a trophy, hopping victoriously.

Phoenix looked up at Emperia. She was incredulous.

9

For the first time, the Emperial GameBots suffered a defeat against human force of will. The Vice President wasted no time seizing upon the emotional change in the atmosphere.

Mae rose above the main gate standing atop a silver CloudRunner. The sleek vehicle resembled a vintage Vespa scooter, with blue HoverJets on small wings beneath her feet keeping the craft airborne. Mae spoke into her LifeRing, her voice echoing throughout the stadium. "Congratulations, Team Human! Now, a surprise for our winning quarterback, we've arranged for his Emperial truck to join the festivities!"

Phoenix watched Franklin roll out of the main gate, looking snazzy with a fresh coat of red paint and newly polished chrome. "Congrats, ol' chum!" he said in his Brooklyn accent.

Phoenix laughed. "You're lookin' sharp, buddy!"

"Thanks. Now, jump in, quick-like."

The stadium announcer spoke. "Everyone remain seated. The previous play is under review..."

"Are you kidding me?" said Halzac.

"Review these!" Stew yelled, grabbing his privates.

"Security, remove the truck from the field," the announcer continued.

Mayhem broke loose. Emperia stood up from her seat, rigid as she issued rapid-fire commands through her LifeRing.

Mae flew the CloudRunner across the field. Azalea and Lars helped Halzac hop to a back seat of the truck. Phoenix was already at the driver's seat.

"Franklin, follow!" Mae called out.

"Attention Team Human," the announcer said. "Exit the truck immediately."

Emperia was now screaming into her LifeRing.

Phoenix tapped impatiently on the steering wheel, noticing Franklin wasn't allowing him to control the vehicle. "Let's go, Frankie!"

"I'll do the driving for now," Franklin said as he revved his engine, now sounding more like a jet than a truck.

"Wait, where's Stew?" yelled Phoenix above the noise, looking around at Halzac, Lars and Azalea.

"He scurried through a maintenance door," said Halzac. "I'm wondering if I should've done the same..."

Mae hovered above them on her CloudRunner. Speaking into her LifeRing, her words echoed throughout the stadium. "My fellow Americans, what I'm about to say will shock some, while others are already aware of what is happening to our government. Emperia is trying to hijack the election system. Her aim is to consolidate power unlike any president before her. This is not what the Founding Fathers intended, and I will not let it happen. Therefore, I must leave. But when I return, freedom will prevail." The audience, stupefied by her words, didn't know how to react.

Emperia shook with rage, blurting out, "Treasonous liar! Arrest her!"

Mae sped toward the front gate. Franklin followed, but it was blocked by a brigade of MotorMaidens with laser rifles drawn. Phoenix glanced in the rearview screen and saw Emperial Guards brandishing BrightSwords.

"I guess Stew was the smart one after all," said Halzac.

As Emperial forces closed in on them, the truck shook with a bang. Everyone jumped in their seats. "Incoming!" yelled Azalea. But Phoenix realized the disturbance wasn't from an outside assault, but from Franklin's own systems. There was another thump and a powerful roar from the vehicle's undercarriage.

"Boosters engaged!" Franklin said.

"What boosters?' said Phoenix, looking over the dashboard for new controls. With a thrust of g-force, Franklin shot into the air, far above the stadium walls, following Mae's CloudRunner eastward toward the ocean.

Among the shocked crowd, nobody was as stunned as Emperia. A feeling of betrayal swept through her. Eyes bulging, she tried to remain calm, deliberating how to proceed. She raised her LifeRing to her tense lips. "Track the vehicles leaving the stadium. Do not engage. Find out where they're going." She lowered her ring and looked over to her android bodyguard. "Your assessment, Vincent?"

His eyebrows lifted as his lips curled down to convey compassion. "It's puzzling. She had everything to gain with the new voting system."

"She'll be held accountable."

"Attention," said the stadium announcer. "Team Human is disqualified. Early departure prohibited. Forfeit! Emperial GameBots: victors!"

Music blared and the bots launched into a victory dance, oblivious to the unexpected circumstances. Scattered amid the audience's confused applause were undertones of booing, searing into Emperia's ears like tongues of fire.

ACT 2

10

Any illusion Phoenix had that life would ever be the same ended over the Atlantic Ocean. Familiar remnants of his regular world morphed into the surreal as Franklin carried Team Human through moonlit clouds.

Looking out at Mae leading them atop the CloudRunner, he realized how dire the political situation must be for her to take such radical action. Mae was not an escapist. While continually underestimated because of her blonde locks and charming air, she was a struggling idealist with a rationale for every move.

Rumbling through the sky, Phoenix tried to picture what kind of life awaited him beyond the Emperial grid. One thing he knew for sure: if he bit the apple that night with Morgan, now he consumed it to the core.

"This is what I'm talkin' about!" hollered Azalea, anything but pensive as they soared through the sky.

"Since when do Emperial trucks fly?" asked Halzac.

"Care to explain, Franklin?" said Phoenix.

Franklin's voice boomed from the dash. "It was Rudeen, she hooked me up with a killer custom job."

Halzac looked over at Phoenix. "Who's Rudeen?"

"My Role Officer."

Halzac was impressed. "Whoa, you'da man!" He stroked his mustache. "A woman in high places..."

"Hold tight, everyone!" said Franklin, boosting his jets to catch up with Mae. After hours passing over the ocean, a warning chime sounded from the dashboard. Phoenix saw Franklin's fuel gauge running low. Lightning flashed ahead, and for the first time, the turbulent waters looked less like freedom and more like a watery grave.

"Brace for landing," said Franklin.

But with no actual land in site, apprehensions ramped up another notch. "Land where?" said Halzac looking out at the endless sea. "Don't tell me this thing's a boat too!"

"It better be, 'cause I can't swim!" said Azalea.

Descending toward the surface, the waves crashed, creating a thick mist amid crackles of lightning. The dashboard went dim as Franklin's power neared exhaustion.

Lars yelped, putting his face in his hands.

"It's going to be all right, big guy," Azalea consoled him. "We ain't goin' out like this."

As Phoenix stared down at the violent waves, something enormous emerged from the ocean resembling the shell of a giant turtle. "Wait a minute..."

They watched as a gigantic curved structure rose to the surface, resembling a monstrous painter turtle with lights shining through the translucent plates of its shell. Water flowed down its colorful sides, creating massive waves.

"If it ain't a battleship-sized turtle!" said Azalea.

One of the hexagonal plates on the vessel slid open. They watched Mae maneuver the CloudRunner over to the opening and descend into the ship.

"Okay, Franklin, you got this," said Phoenix as the fuel gauge blinked red.

Franklin hovered just above the open plate of the submarine, but the wind picked up making it difficult to keep steady. "We're out of power!" said Phoenix, as a platform rose from the opening to catch them.

After they were safely lowered into the vessel, the team shared a sigh of relief. Phoenix stepped out of the truck, seeing a ring of lights illuminating the walls lined with maintenance equipment. Large arrows glowed on the floor for directing both people and vehicles.

Lars and Azalea helped Halzac out of the back seat as Mae stepped off the CouldRunner.

"Where in Her Nation are we?" said Azalea.

"No longer in Her Damn Nation," said Halzac.

"We're in an experimental sub," said Mae. "It will take us to safety. But first, we must get rid of all devices. Time to cut the cord to Emperia." She removed her LifeRing and hurled it out the open plate above her. They could hear it clang as it rolled down the ship's shell before falling into the ocean.

Azalea shrugged her shoulders, then did the same with her ring. Phoenix looked down at his LifeWatch and noticed the screen had changed, flashing an image of red chains around the word *Fugitive*. He unbuckled the watch and threw it out the hatch, hearing it bounce along the sub's outer plates before plunging into the sea. Without a word, Halzac and Lars also cast away their connection to Emperia.

A moment of anxious silence followed, everyone used to the devices performing so many wonders for them.

They felt naked, but free.

Shaking them from their thoughts, the plate above closed with a thud, forming an air-tight seal. Phoenix felt his ears pop, then the pull of gravity in his stomach as the sub sank into the ocean's unfathomable depths.

11

As Emperial forces combed land and sea for the runaway Vice President, Team Human cruised the ocean's depths in the turtle-shaped submarine.

Leaving Franklin and the CloudRunner on the landing bay, they took an elevator to the sub's lobby. The comfortable cavern featured a tortoise-shell ceiling with glowing tiles that slowly alternated colors, illuminating the soft wood floor, bar and cabinetry. An older man of Indian descent in a white coat greeted them, pushing an empty wheelchair. He was a round man with a warm presence and broad smile.

Mae embraced him. "Doctor Bandhu! It's been too long. Thank you for your generosity."

"Vice President O'Herra, oh my," he said, returning her warmth.

Lars helped Halzac into the wheelchair. "My knee thanks you, Doc."

"You're very welcome." Bandhu looked over at everyone. "It gladdens my heart to see you all. Congratulations on beating those dreadful GameBots. It's about time the world saw good ol' human wit overcoming mechanical monstrosity."

Over the next days and nights, the Doctor helped them quiet their minds and recharge their bodies. One evening, they relaxed together on a tan carpet in a white oval room. Bandhu sat crosslegged, spine straight with a calm smile. "Emperia is like a force of nature. To challenge her requires bravery. On your perilous journey, beware of the greatest adversary: fear.

Our own fears can be as strong as any opponent. But there's an easy way out, an ancient remedy, a powerful elixir which I'd like to share with you..."

"Bring it on," said Azalea.

"Yeah, I'll take a chug," said Halzac,

The Doctor giggled. "It's not in a bottle or anything you can see. It's something already within you, something you've owned since birth... Your breath."

Halzac shrugged his shoulders. ""I'm already breathing, Doc. How's that gonna get me buzzed?"

Bandhu smiled. "The question is: *how* are you breathing? Is it fast or slow? Shallow or deep? Even or choppy? Our breath reflects our state of mind and can even predict our lifespan. Watch your breath, even for a few minutes, and see yourself lifted from the mental maze of mirrors where worry lurks. From there, one can advance, using breath exercises not just for calming, but for inner strength, sharpness of intellect, quieting of the pulse, even for reaching cosmic states that bring you closer to the force sustaining us."

"Aha! So you *can* get high," said Halzac.

"Doctor," said Mae, emulating his sitting pose. "How about a breath for long life."

He nodded gently. "Personally, I like to listen to my breath like the ocean waves. Each breath in: a wave rolling onto the shore. Each breath out: a wave flowing back to the sea. With eyes closed, it's like teleporting to the beach. Meanwhile, life-extending endorphins are released from the body's own medicine chest."

Azalea laughed. "You crazy, Doc, like crazy cool. How about a breath for high-stress situations like these peeps be puttin' me through."

"Ah, for the triumphant Team Human, here's one to recharge your batteries and bring inner peace. Breathe in gently through the nose, filling the belly. Hold for a few seconds, imagine a healing light filling the belly, spreading joyful energy throughout the body. Then, breathe out, *Ahh*..."

They all gave it a try. After some silence, Azalea sighed with a deep *"Ahh"* and collapsed onto Lars. "Yeah, baby..."

As they sat in stillness, Phoenix watched Bandhu with his blissful smile, eyes closed, appearing almost luminescent. Then, as if Bandhu knew Phoenix was watching, he spoke softly. "Phoenix, there's something you should know... You may come into possession of a powerful innovation, one of which the world has never known."

Halzac was more curious than Phoenix. "What kind of innovation we talkin' here, Doc?"

"A thing of legends and folktales, yet made real with technology ... a new kind of sword that powers itself from energy of the human heart."

Lars thumped his chest with his fist. "Aye!"

Bandhu smiled. "Like the strong-hearted Lars, we all cast a field of energy around us. Ancient sages knew it, and later, scientists proved it. In fact, the electromagnetic field of the human heart could fill an entire room."

"Impressive," said Halzac. "But why does Phoenix get this sword?"

Bandhu chuckled. "I'm not certain he will. We don't always fulfill our destiny. Sometimes, fate gets in the way."

"Hmm," said Mae. "What's the difference?"

"Destiny is when we achieve our soul's mission. Fate is when we let life's illusions get in the way."

Phoenix seemed perplexed and already on the verge of

overwhelmed. "Why me? I mean, what will I need to do?"

"Nothing for now, just keep choosing acts of compassion, generosity and love. Such virtuous acts raise the heart's energy, which in turn increases power to the sword."

Mae was intrigued. "It seems such a weapon would be useless to the wicked, who lack virtue."

"That's the hope," said Bandhu.

Mae smiled with admiration. "Was this your inspiration?"

"I imagined it, but it was an old friend who turned the dream into reality. He's the one you should find on the island..."

"You must mean Shandao," said Mae.

"The one and only."

Halzac laughed. "The old coot's hiding out on an island?"

Bandhu smiled. "Aging like a redwood tree."

The next morning, Phoenix awoke in his small cabin. He instinctively checked for his LifeWatch, forgetting it was likely wrapped in seaweed along the ocean floor.

After a gentle tap at the door, Mae peeked into the cabin. Seeing him awake, she smiled. "A whale just passed by my window."

"A good sign, I hope..."

"Today is the day we reach our destination, an island paradise, actually. But we have work to do. Let's just pray Shandao is really there, our best hope to stop Emperia."

"I've been wondering, Emperia has charisma, eloquence, gravitas..."

"My," interrupted Mae. "I didn't know you were such an admirer."

"Well, I mean, why does she need to rig the system to get her way? Doesn't she get it anyway?"

Mae stared at Phoenix a moment with coldness in her blue eyes. "For some, power only creates craving for more power. It's the deadliest of diseases. If Emperia enacts her new voting system, the America we know is over. It will be a transfer of power to her chosen few." She locked eyes with him. "Phoenix, when we get to the island, I want to share an idea that could save our country. It seems radical, but it's actually a return to our roots."

Before she could continue, Azalea burst through the door. "Land ho, maties!" she said with a toothy grin. "Got a date with a tropical breeze!"

Halzac waltzed in behind her, bright-eyed and lively with a freshly trimmed mustache. "Haul it upstairs, people! Doc's got grub hot and *now*."

"Knee's better, huh?" said Phoenix.

"Last night the Doc slapped the crap out of it, oil and herbed it... *Bam*, woke up like new."

Azalea scoffed. "Was he fixin' your knee or makin' a salad?"

"I don't care. It worked. He also showed me a way to keep the joints flexed." He stepped behind Azalea and kicked her in the rear.

"Ow!" She chased him out of the cabin yelling, "Now, watch me whoop your ass!"

Phoenix chuckled. "There go our fellow revolutionaries..."

Mae sighed. "We may be a motley crew, but I've never met a more lucky bunch. Few forces are more powerful than luck, because it's another form of grace."

12

As the sub broke through the surface of the water, sunlight flooded the captain's bridge. Team Human gathered around Bandhu, control panels and screens surrounding a pair of windows like eyes in the head of the mechanized turtle.

After days in the deep ocean, the energetic radiance of daylight made Phoenix squint. As his eyes adjusted, two mountainous islands came into view.

Bandhu walked over to a docking bay where a shiny gray lifeboat hung by cables. He walked down a few steps and rested his hand on the bow. "This will get you to the island."

Phoenix was confused. "What about Franklin?"

"Your truck must stay. He'll be safe here," said Bandhu.

Azalea didn't like the idea. "Wait, you gonna leave us stranded on an island with only a little boat?"

"Maybe Franklin could follow us over," said Phoenix.

"Yeah," said Azalea. "Homie can fly."

"Franklin is a computerized being, a robot on wheels," said Bandhu. "The people here don't like robots. They call them metal demons ... and refer to Emperia as their Electric Queen."

A wry smile crept across Mae's face. "She always did fancy herself a royal."

Halzac shrugged. "What about weapons, you know, self-defense?"

71

"That won't be necessary, and would give the wrong impression," said Bandhu. "They should recognize you and provide sanctuary. Remember, this is an enlightened group of people who *chose* to depart from technology and live among nature, merging ancestral traditions to practice them in peace. Tread lightly."

As everyone absorbed this, the Doctor looked up at an intercom speaker. "Oliver, open up and say *Ah*."

A giant hatch at the end of the dock bay opened like a mouth. "Ahhh," said a deep yet friendly voice as balmy sea air drifted into the room.

"So, this thing talks?" said Halzac.

"Why wouldn't he?" said Bandhu. "Oliver, meet Team Human."

"Hello, there," said Oliver. "I must say, I thoroughly enjoyed watching you kick those GameBots to the curb. I may be a bot, but I was all in for Team Human."

"It's a pleasure to meet you," said Mae. "Your elegant engineering and naturally inspired design live up to reputation."

"I didn't know I had a reputation."

"Quite so, among the few who know about you," Mae said before turning to the Doctor. "Thank you both for transporting us here safely."

Bandhu took Mae's hand. "May you find success on your quest. The lifeboat is yours now. Don't start the motor. They won't like that. There are sails in a cabinet but it's a short trek, perfect for the paddles. They'll get you there without appearing a threat. Now, Oliver and I need to get back underwater. It's not safe for us up here."

Oliver activated a crank connected to the cables, lowering the boat into the water. "You'll find the lifeboat equipped with emergency flotation devices, flares, fishing gear, and – if needed – enough food and water to last five people twenty-one days. Farewell friends."

"Thank you, Oliver," said Mae.

"Thanks, Ollie!" said Azalea. "And I'm diggin' on that sexy voice!"

Lars grimaced with jealousy. "Get over here," she said, pulling him close. "You gonna protect me on that island?" He grunted affectionately as she kissed his cheek.

Mae was the first to climb into the vessel. Everyone boarded smoothly, except Lars who made the boat pitch beneath his weight. He nearly fell on Azalea before she helped him gain his balance. After all were situated, Bandhu pushed the boat with his foot, floating it out of Oliver's mouth to the sea.

Phoenix and Halzac were the first to grab paddles. As Oliver sank underwater, oozing with bubbles, they made their way toward the island.

Phoenix noticed the inhabitants of the island were already on their way toward them. Five canoes loaded with men paddled furiously, chanting in low voices.

"You sure they're expecting us?" said Halzac "'Cause they look pissed!"

The dugout canoes were carved from massive tree trunks with vaulted bows painted to resemble reptilian creatures, a sharp contrast to the mundane boat holding Phoenix and his friends. The men's faces were painted as fiercely as their boats, with sun-baked muscles slashing the oars through the water.

Phoenix couldn't help but catch a few glares. As they circled, spiraling waves rocked the lifeboat.

Mae stood up, addressing them clearly and respectfully. "Greetings, friends. We've come in peace, seeking sanctuary."

"No friends here!" one hollered.

"Go back!" shouted another.

An older man spoke in an authoritative voice. "We have no knowledge of who you are."

"Great," said Halzac, who looked back for Oliver, but the friendly sub was long gone.

"We are enemies of Emperia and her robots," declared Mae.

One of the canoes darted toward them and collided against the side of the lifeboat. Lars grabbed the painted bow angrily and pushed it away. The men drew axes, crossbows and spears. Azalea grabbed Lars. "Chill, big guy!"

Another canoe collided with the boat. "You say you're enemies of the Electric Queen and her minions," an elder said. "But you arrived from the mouth of a robot. Even this boat is wired with dark mind!" He raised his ax and smashed the navigation screen on the ship's stern.

"Come on, now!" said Azalea, starting to huff. "You won't like me when I'm mad."

The elder lowered his ax. "We shall discuss this on land." Escorted by the canoes, Phoenix and Halzac paddled the lifeboat to shore.

On the beach, Team Human found themselves surrounded by men and women in the trees, peering from the bordering forest, wading along the shoreline.

A heavyset warrior with leather straps over his chest approached. He held a spear adorned with feathers, the sharp tip shimmering under the sun.

Mae waved her hand gently. "I am Mae. This is Azalea, Halzac, Lars and Phoenix."

"Phoenix?" said the warrior. All of them took a keen interest in Phoenix. One of them threw down his spear, and

74

knelt below him. As Phoenix looked around puzzled, the man burst out laughing. The others laughed along, some of them howling in amusement.

"Him? The Phoenix?" the warrior said, pointing his finger in Phoenix's face, who slapped the warrior's hand. Before a fight could ensue, a loud chime rang. Everyone stared up at the sky.

Phoenix looked up to see a girl standing perfectly balanced on a branch about twenty feet above them, dressed in a silver and black tunic, wearing a mask made of an Embot's faceplate painted with orange and black stripes. She leapt from the branch, doing a flip and landing in front of Mae. Removing her mask, she revealed her teenage face, shoulder-length black hair and sharp eyes with wide cheekbones. "Welcome to Chandora, unity of mountain and sea. I am Rhain." She turned to her people, who seemed surprised that she welcomed them. "This is Team Human, who defeated the metal demons. Treat them with respect."

"But Rhain," the warrior said. "They claim he's The Phoenix."

"His name is Phoenix. They didn't say he's The Phoenix from the legends of our ancestors. Again, let's show respect to our guests."

Mae approached Rhain and bowed. "Thank you, Rhain. Your hospitality is most appreciated. We have come for sanctuary on your precious island as refugees escaping Emperia."

"It is my honor to welcome you and the others, Mae O'Herra." Rhain spoke with a maturity beyond her years. "I possess one satellite radio powered by the sun, our only link to the outside world. I listened to the game and was inspired by your victory against the odds."

Azalea looked around. "So, how did a tot like you get to be the big shot around here?"

"My father helped organize various communities to unite here to live as our ancestors did. But the unification efforts weren't always smooth. Divisions and rivals arose. In a heated argument, my father lost his life. After deliberation and a vision from our shaman, I took his place to guide us forward. Since then, we've been one people at peace, different but united in reverence of nature."

"I'm sorry for your loss," said Mae. "But congratulate you on receiving such an honor."

"Thank you. Now, I have a question. Why did you choose our island?"

"We have one simple mission here, to find a man named Shandao," said Mae. "I was told he might be staying here."

Rhain shook her head. "I know nothing about a Shandao."

Mae couldn't hide her disappointment. It was the first time Phoenix saw a break in her confidence. She turned to him, whispering. "There is one explanation. Shandao is Emperia's father. It's possible he hasn't revealed himself to them."

As the orange sun melted into indigo waves, people mingled and danced in a giant circle around a fire. At one point, Azalea stole the show with her fast-flying gyrations, which quickly caught on with both young and old. Near the shore, Lars took part in wrestling matches among some warriors. He managed to pin down one of the more revered fighters, earning their respect. Halzac and Mae enjoyed the exotic food and tropical drinks at a round banquet table.

Phoenix sat up on a hill overlooking it all. There were no bots monitoring everyone, no gadgets distracting everyone, just men and women celebrating as equals. It all seemed so natural, so unlike the insulated life he knew back in civilization. He realized the people here lived spontaneously, without striving and scheming for an imagined future payoff. They lived each moment to the fullest in a community of peace, amid the generous gifts of Mother Nature instead of the binding grid of the Electric Queen.

13

The Milky Way marched toward the moon like a procession of candle bearers. Atop the Pink House, the face of the moon reflected upon the glassy surface of a koi pond. A sobbing, swooning tune radiated from a golden harp.

Emperia strummed the harp with eyes closed, creating melodies of pining and regret. She wore a silk gown inspired by the American flag, with silvery stars and red stripes draped down her leg. White flowers adorned her hair like a crown.

Deliberately, her fingers swept the strings as the despondent dirge took form. She swooped up the scale as the pace quickened, plucking with rapid-fire precision, stomping the harp's pedals like weapons of war. At the climax, the pond's surface rippled in cascading circles, and the koi jumped and danced. Finally, with a gentle sweep of the strings, she drifted down to the resolution where chords lingered like clouds. The pond became still again as she returned to the melancholic opening, notes evoking deep violet and blood red hues that gave the moon its howling face.

When she stopped playing, she gazed skyward, her powder-white skin glowed under the stars. Her red lips quivered as she whispered. "My father, why did you leave me?"

Only silence answered, until the gentlemanly voice of Vincent lifted the mood. "Pardon me, Madam President." He stood in the arched gateway of the rooftop garden in his metallic tuxedo. "I bring good news."

The presence of her robotic confidant pierced through her inner fog like a sunbeam. "Yes, Vincent?"

"We made progress in our search for the rebels. Underwater drones tracked an unidentified submarine that made a brief stop at an island in the Caribbean Sea. There is a high probability we located our runaway vice president, and perhaps a rebel base too."

Emperia's gaze sharpened. All sadness left her body. Confidence bloomed in her expression. She stood up from the harp, straight as a pillar, clasping her hands. "Prepare three warships. Let's show the world what happens to traitors."

14

At dawn, the stars over the beach vanished into atmospheric blue. Phoenix awoke and watched the first rays of sunlight ricochetting off the crests of waves. As he stood before the rising sun, a shadow passed over him: the silhouette of a husky animal prowling along the water. Thoughts of the wolf he wrestled in the scrapyard filled his mind. But this beast walked with the methodically chosen steps of a feline.

It stopped and stared over at him. Phoenix felt his pulse rise, realizing the thing could be looking for breakfast. But the beast turned its head and continued treading along the shore, more like a wanderer than a predator.

Fascinated, Phoenix kept to the edge of the forest, following quietly behind, moving from tree to tree. Finally, the animal walked onto a small peninsula of sand, allowing a clear view. Phoenix beheld a magnificent snow leopard with a white coat and black spots. The strange appearance startled Phoenix, causing him to trip over a protruding tree root. When he stood up, the leopard stared back at him.

Turning toward the ocean, the animal abruptly walked into the sea. Phoenix assumed it went fishing, so he waited behind a tree for a couple minutes, but the leopard never re-emerged.

Phoenix stepped out from the forest and waded in the water, trying to peer into the depths. He figured the creature should have come back for air by now, but somehow it was still underwater.

Anxiety rose with each passing second the leopard stayed underwater. Sitting on a stump, he waited, completely perplexed. He began to question his own sanity, wondering if his mind was faulty without the direction of his LifeWatch.

He heard a noise down the shore and looked over to see Halzac charging into the water with a spear. Wondering if maybe Halzac saw the leopard, Phoenix headed toward him.

As he approached, Halzac cried out, "Bam! Got one!" He emerged with a large catfish on the end of the spear. Halzac noticed the strange look in Phoenix's eyes, and lowered the fish. "What's itchin' your brain?"

"Did you just see a leopard out here?" He waited for the response like his mental stability depended on it.

Halzac quickly scanned the beach, clutching his spear, but saw nothing. He looked back at Phoenix skeptically. "You drank too much of that palm juice last night, didn't you?"

"I followed him down the beach. He swam in the water then disappeared."

"Hmm... A leopard in the Caribbean? Fat chance, unless somebody brought it here. And if they did, leopards don't normally go *poof* in the ocean." He shook his head.

Phoenix's spine quivered. He felt dislocated from reality, like when he watched Morgan dive off the roof of the club and vanish without a trace.

"Go take a swim. Clear your head," said Halzac.

Phoenix gazed back at the ocean, scanning in a renewed search.

"Or better yet, grab a spear and catch some food. Like Emperia says, make yourself useful!"

Phoenix went back to where he last saw the leopard, checking the sand for paw prints, but the rising tide had erased the past. Finally, he abandoned the search and launched himself into a wave.

15

A man used to drifting across the globe, Halzac felt at home body-surfing back to shore. Floating along with a spear, a grin crossed his lips, knowing he caught enough to feed his friends. Emerging from the ocean, he clutched the spear like a savage lumbering onto foreign land.

Up ahead, he spotted a sandy cove surrounded by palm trees. There, he gazed upon a woman lying beside a crystal clear stream. He approached slowly, slyly.

The woman reclined on a colorful hand-woven blanket, wearing a yellow sarong. She surrendered to the blazing sun, hair wrapped in a silvery silk scarf shielding her eyes. Her shiny, curvy leg peaked through the slit of her sarong. Every detail of her sumptuous figure captured Halzac's attention, as she seemed unaware of his presence.

He sank his spear into the sand and stepped closer, sweating sea water.

Unfazed, she slid the scarf away from her face, revealing herself to be Mae. To Halzac's surprise, her eyes reflected his desire. He knelt beside her, knowing not to utter a word that could easily offend this near-goddess. She lifted her chin a degree and tilted toward him.

A freewheeling man of action, he could never pass up such an opportunity, and so he went in for the kill... Their lips locked, like two pieces of a puzzle. He never felt such a surge of emotion. Of all the women he ever kissed, none were as sweet as this.

Before things could escalate, Azalea's voice rang out. "Dinner! Get it while the gettin's good!"

They both had to laugh, the humor only adding to the charm of the moment. Walking along a sandy trail together, they followed the spicy smoke. When they reached the camp, Lars arrived with armfuls of coconuts. Azalea squeezed lime over the fish, which sizzled on a makeshift grill with pineapple and slivers of pumpkin.

Rhain appeared in a brilliant red and yellow tunic, adding an aura of authority that made up for her youth. "I see you've had no problem adapting."

"Stick around, Rhain, we got plenty," said Azalea.

"I'd be honored."

"You know, I could live here," said Halzac. "Swim, fish, eat my catch, crash under the stars."

Phoenix arrived, pale-faced as he staggered into the camp, collapsing onto the sand.

"What's up with Fee? said Azalea. "You look like you saw a ghost."

"Yeah, a ghost-leopard," said Halzac.

This grabbed Rhain's attention. "You saw the leopard?"

Phoenix stood, a glimmer of hope in his eyes. "I saw a snow leopard on the beach this morning. Tell me I'm not crazy."

Rhain's jaw dropped, her eyes widened, now showing her youth. "I can't believe you saw him."

"So, he's *real*!" said Phoenix, a weight lifted from his mind.

Rhain didn't return Phoenix's enthusiasm, staring downcast. "Others have seen him. I've only heard tall tales from kids." She looked up at Phoenix, wanting to hear more.

"I followed him until he swam underwater. But he never came back up, just vanished."

"Vanished?" said Mae. "Sounds like some kind of bot."

"Which means we're under surveillance," said Halzac.

"Maybe the leopard isn't hostile," said Mae. "Shandao draws inspiration for his creations from wildlife. If he's here, maybe this creature is with him."

"Actually," said Rhain, "There is a strange presence here. Our shaman found something hidden in a mountain cave. Perhaps it belongs to the one you're seeking."

16

Rhain led Team Human into a dense forest. Sand turned to pine needles along the trail, crackling beneath their feet, filling the air with a minty scent. Moss grew like beards over the faces of ancient trees.

Rhain strayed from the main trail, leading them down a narrow path trodden by animals. They crossed a stream on a bridge of stepping stones, arriving at the base of a steep hill. Vines grew along the upward path for support.

After a rugged ascent, they reached a granite plateau overlooking the wind-rippled sand merging into the deep blue ocean.

Rhain led them into the mouth of a large cave where they came upon a green HoverCopter. Aerodynamic to an extreme, HoverCopters were shaped like a drop of water falling horizontally. No longer needing propellers since the dawn of HoverJets, they flew in utter silence.

"How long has it been here?" asked Mae, examining the white letters on the door reading, *Emperial Transport.*

"Our shaman discovered it a few months ago while gathering herbs."

Halzac walked up to the door and began fiddling with a control panel. "Let's see if the access-scanner works..." He placed his thumb on the round screen and two beams of light passed over his face.

"Access denied," a female voice spoke firmly from the

panel.

"Give me a BrightKnife. I'll get in," said Halzac.

Mae shook her head. "A BrightKnife couldn't breach a HoverCopter. And if this is Shandao's, we should protect it. He's potentially our ally, also in exile from Emperia."

Halzac wouldn't let it go. "We should at least try to see what's inside! I've busted into more secure vessels than this. Come on, VP, I know you got a knife. Let me take a crack at it!"

Mae finally silenced him with an icy glare.

Meanwhile, Phoenix placed his thumb on the access-scanner. Beams of light illuminated his face. This time the voice said, "Access granted." Hearing a bolt unlock inside the door, he looked back at everyone, as surprised as they were.

"You goin' in or what?" said Halzac.

Phoenix opened the hatch and stepped into the vessel. Immediately the door closed behind him. Climbing into the cockpit, he looked over the controls. The black and yellow dashboard was strikingly similar to Franklin's. On the tan upholstery of the copilot's seat, he saw a short black hair. He lifted it, examining its coarseness, wondering if it might be the hair of an animal.

The dashboard lit up as the hoarse voice of a man well advanced in years spoke. "Greetings, young one. I am looking for someone with the speed to follow the elusive leopard roaming these islands. Find where he stays, and you find me."

"Is this Shandao?" said Phoenix, but there was no response. "Hello?" Still nothing. Whoever the man was, Phoenix found his challenge intriguing. Just before he climbed out of the cockpit, a button on the dash glowed green. He pressed it and a cargo hatch opened at the base of the copter.

Stepping outside, Phoenix saw Halzac lift a BoltRifle out of the hatch. "Now, we're talkin'," he said with the excitement of a kid getting a birthday gift. The silvery rifle was sleek but bulky with a golden lightning bolt painted on the side. He pulled out another one and gave it to Lars. "Don't zap your face off, big guy."

"Wait!" said Rhain. "My people cannot see these. It would cause confusion and anger. Please keep them here where they are safe."

Halzac looked over at Mae, who nodded in agreement with Rhain. Lars placed the rifle back in the cargo container, but Halzac kept his. "I'll hide it myself. Might need it in a pinch."

Mae rolled her eyes. Rhain shook her head as she pushed the hatch shut. "Keep it well hidden."

Phoenix walked over to Mae and Rhain to show them the strand of black hair. "Found this on the co-pilot's seat..."

"Let's see," said Rhain, taking the hair and examining it closely. "Could be from our spotted leopard."

"The challenge is to find where the leopard stays," said Phoenix. "At least, according to the guy who spoke through the dash. He said if I find the leopard, I'll find him."

Elated, Mae put her hands on his shoulders. "Sounds like you just made our first connection with Shandao. Now, we'll all be looking for that leopard."

Leaving the cave, Mae noticed Halzac unlocking the safety switch on the BoltRifle, flipping it around, playing with the controls. "It's not a toy," she scolded him.

"Just trying to make sure it works, my dear." He took aim at a tall, craggy pine not far from them. Before anyone could object, he squeezed the trigger. A flashing bolt blasted the tree, enveloping it in a web of electricity. The force of the strike caused the tree to topple. One large branch fell like a spear toward Azalea, but Lars pulled her to safety. As the limb stabbed the ground, smaller branches flew out like shrapnel, one striking Halzac in the head. "Damn!" he yelled.

"A message from the tree." said Rhain with a frown.

Halzac rubbed his head. "Received."

Azalea kissed Lars, then glared at Halzac like a bull seeing red. "I wanna *talk* to you!" She began to chase him into the cave, but stopped, waving her hand dismissively. "Oh, what's the point..."

Halzac crept back out with an apologetic gaze. "My bad, Zale!"

"You're a damn fool! We all are, here in paradise but we just wanna go back and mess with the Electric Bitch. Well, *I'm out*!" She flung her hands in the air and turned around to walk down the mountainside.

"Azalea!" Mae stepped in front of her. "There's a reason we made it this far, *together*."

"We beat the GameBots, Princess. That was *my* mission. Anything more is suicide, if you ask me."

"Truth be told," said Halzac. "The fishing here is, well, damn good. Maybe Zale's got a point."

Mae shook her head. "The sun here is strong. The air is sweet. But there's a higher calling, freedom to preserve." She held out her hand, acknowledging the island's stunning scenery. "In such a place, the temptation is strong to forget that our homeland is under siege by its own leader."

Rhain nodded. "If it was up to me, you could make your home here. But my people would have to vote on it. I guide day-to-day affairs, but we vote on big decisions, instead of relying on one person who may have bias."

Mae nodded admiringly. "I truly love your style of democracy. And no vote will be needed. Once we connect with Shandao, we'll be on our way."

"Thank you for understanding. My people really don't want to bring Emperia back to our island."

"She's been here before?" said Mae.

"Yes. It's time you saw the surreal scene left from her last visit..."

17

In a forest clearing under the scorching sun, six Embots aged like monuments of a lost civilization. Tree pollen and cocoons stuck to their bones. Rust oozed from the seams of their polished polymers and mixed metals. Vines grappled the bot's ankles, crawling upward in preparation for an earthly entombment.

Phoenix marveled at the irony of the android's fate, not in battle but beneath the tiny feet of ivy. He noticed another Embot missing its faceplate, no doubt the one Rhain wore when she first greeted them. The bot's bugged-out eyes were left surrounded by a mesh of circuitry.

"They came without warning," said Rhain. "Combed the island and examined our children. We complied with their wishes, answered questions and let them collect DNA. But while they kept busy, I launched a quiet attack from the trees."

"Whoa," said Halzac. "You took these out yourself, Rhain?"

"With the help of a little potion... It all started one night when strange lights surrounded the hut of our shaman. He stepped outside to see something whirling in the air and then sweep away. Left on the ground were three vials, each containing a clear liquid. A sketch attached to the vials showed how to drop the liquid onto androids to destroy them internally.

"Sure enough, six days later, the metal demons arrived. They collected leaf samples, asked odd questions, took hair clippings from our children. The whole time, I watched from the trees, carefully raining down the liquid on the invaders."

"Raining? Ha!" laughed Azalea. "You got that right."

"Then what?" said Halzac.

"Nothing at first. But later, the potion must have eaten through the seams of their armor. For the next day, some of them began to malfunction, speaking gibberish, bumping into trees."

Halzac chuckled. "Like a bunch of drunks."

"The malfunctioning bots gathered here, speaking incoherently to each other. We didn't know what they were doing or why. All the functioning bots were ordered off the island, leaving these behind."

"Probably worried they'd infect the others," said Mae. "Yet careless to leave malfunctioning bots among people who oppose technology."

"Well, luckily their energy reserves depleted after a few days. Here they've remained."

"The potion must've come from Shandao," said Mae. "Who else would have known the bots were coming, or how to get rid of them?"

Halzac walked up and down the row of disabled Embots, examining them. "All I can say is, nice work, Rhain. You've given us an opportunity here. We've got some busted bots, some crusty rots, and one BoltRifle." He grinned, his mustache spreading out like wings. "Target practice!"

Everyone turned to Rhain. She shrugged her shoulders. "It's better than blowing up innocent trees."

Azalea walked up to Halzac and grabbed the rifle from his hand. "You had your fun, sucker. *My* turn..."

Everyone huddled behind a cluster of boulders. Azalea stared down one of the bots through the scope.

"Squeeze nice and easy," said Halzac. "It'll do the work."

Azalea glared at him. "I know how to shoot, potato head!" She refocused her attention, keeping her aim steady as she pulled the trigger. She struck the android's chest. The burst of electricity crackled through its bones, giving it enough juice to shout in a high-pitched voice, "Halt or die!"

Phoenix had to laugh, hearing the dreaded phrase sound so ridiculous. The charge looped through the machine, causing it to overheat and finally explode. Everyone crouched behind the boulders as metal bones and burning wire filled the air. When the scene settled, cheering erupted.

Lars was next, and the others followed, not only acquainting themselves with a powerful weapon, but venting some frustration after a lifetime at the mercy of machines.

The sun set through towering pines as the rising roar of crickets ushered in the night. The bots now reduced to smoldering heaps, Team Human gathered around one of the piles like basking in the glow of a bonfire.

Phoenix noticed how relaxed everyone seemed as they sat back telling stories of their past lives under Emperia.

A rustling of leaves on a branch above caught Phoenix's attention. He stood, waving his arms for everyone to be quiet.

Halzac peered through the BoltRifle's scope at the treetops, seeing the silhouette of a large animal leaping from tree to tree. "It's the leopard."

They watched the shadowy figure carefully descend branch by branch before reaching the ground. He approached slowly, moonlight illuminating his silver-gray eyes and spotted coat.

"You're a sleek one!" Azalea said, peeking out from behind

Lars.

Rhain beamed profoundly. "A wish fulfilled."

The animal walked with a royal saunter, now wearing a leather harness with various gadgets attached.

Up close, Phoenix saw a certain wisdom in the creature's calm face. "Hello, my friend."

The leopard nodded, then turned his head. Lights beamed from the harness, creating a hologram amid the crickets and vines. The revolving image showed Mae as she appeared in the game wearing her blue coach's uniform. Words below her declared, *Wanted for Treason.* A female news anchor spoke with stern authority. "The Vice President and members of so-called Team Human are considered armed and dangerous. If you have any information concerning these persons, please contact your local authorities." The hologram displayed close-ups of Phoenix, Halzac, Lars and Azalea as they were last seen in their team jerseys.

"Damn, we be lookin' good!" said Azalea.

As the hologram ended, the leopard stepped back. A blinding flash from a camera on his harness lit up everyone's stunned faces, then the creature darted into the black forest.

Phoenix ran after the fast-flying feline, following the swishing leaves in the leopard's wake. He made it to where the forest meets the shoreline sand, but to his dismay, the tracks led straight into the ocean like last time.

He crouched down to rest, as if the race were lost, when something caught his eye: a faint orange glow below the surface of the sea. Hope renewed, he ran into the water, diving in the direction of the light. He forced himself to open his eyes underwater, something he was never able to do. He could make out a reddish-yellow sphere hovering just above the seafloor.

Scooping water and kicking furiously, he made it to the object. Like a giant grapefruit with translucent skin, it was a two-person submarine. The leopard appeared not far away, swimming gracefully beneath the vessel and crawling up through a hatch on the underbelly.

Phoenix was thrilled to finally understand how the leopard was able to stay underwater.

His will to win the challenge overrode any fear. In his last breath, he reached the hatch. The portal was covered in a pale blue field of light that dried Phoenix completely as he entered the vessel.

The leopard lifted his paw and pressed a green button with humanlike precision. A transparent door slid over the hatch as the ship began gliding effortlessly above the seafloor. Phoenix looked around for a motor or any technology, but only found two buttons, one green and one red. The skin-like exterior seemed to react to the water itself, moving without a sound as if pulled by some sort of sideways gravity.

"Are you taking me to Shandao?" Phoenix asked gently.

When the leopard looked over, Phoenix almost expected words to emanate from his whiskered lips, but instead he just licked his paw like any cat would do.

After watching the seaweed pass for awhile, the leopard pressed the red button and the vessel slowed before coming to a stop. It connected to a tunnel made of the same organic-like material.

Another transparent portal opened and the animal led Phoenix through the tunnel. They walked upward until they rose above sea level, stepping onto a mossy slope at the base of a mountain.

Phoenix looked up to see a series of granite peaks

resembling fingers of a hand reaching heavenward. The scene brought an inexplicable rush of intuition, that mystical well of wisdom flowing deeper than knowledge and experience. He realized the whirlwind of events in his life were all preparing him for this moment.

18

The moon beamed above a round pond fed by two streams rolling over a stone ledge. Dozens of smaller streams reached out from the pond like veins. After a hearty climb up the mountain, the leopard trotted into the small reservoir to quench his thirst.

Phoenix also stepped into the pond. Leaning into the clear flowing waterfall, he drank in the life-giving water.

The feline proceeded to march right through the waterfall, disappearing behind the flow.

Phoenix laughed, struck with wonder by the hidden passage. He walked through too, reaching a cave carpeted with moss. A tunnel led out to a canyon spotted with towering trees and more granite peaks.

Following the leopard through the canyon, Phoenix heard the faint notes of a bamboo flute. The music led them to a mountain pool surrounded by old pines. The leopard's flashlight switched off, the moon providing ample light. By the pool, they saw the source of the music: a cloaked figure playing the instrument. His body swayed as his silvery beard shimmered to the flute's hymn, unaware of any audience.

The song took an upward swing into a climax filled with high-pitched, searing notes fired like colorful arrows. Phoenix noticed fish in the pool jumping to the surface, splashing like cymbals crashing. The tune softened to a melancholic finale and the fish disappeared back into the depths. The man lowered his head as if mourning.

Phoenix was unsure if he should speak, but knew he couldn't just stay silent. "Shandao, is that you?"

The man, jolted by the intrusion, leapt to his feet swiftly. With a swipe of his hand across his cloak, a fiery sword burst forth. "Who's there?" His voice was dark, formidable, commanding. Phoenix knew it was the voice he heard from the HoverCopter's dashboard.

The light of the blazing saber illuminated the man's Asian features, showing the ridges and grooves of the decades. He wore a brown linen robe with golden trim that reflected the sword's light.

"I caught up with your leopard..."

"Phoenix, let me see you better." He thrust his sword forward, shooting an orb of fire that ignited a nearby pile of wood. They saw each other for the first time, Phoenix illuminated by the bonfire, the old man by the fire of his sword.

"So, you're the one we're looking for," said Phoenix.

"Question is: Are you the one?" Shandao pressed a button on the sword and the fiery blade retracted into the hilt.

"You challenged me. Here I am."

"I've been watching you for a while now," said Shandao, approaching. "You've shown strength and speed, even some intelligence. But I still wonder... More is required."

Shandao walked over to the leopard. He slid the hilt of the sword into a sheath attached to the leopard's harness. "Keep her safe, Himalaya."

"*Himalaya*," said Phoenix. He raised the pitch of his voice a notch, like speaking to a young child. "*Where are you from?*"

Shandao chuckled. "Stop talking to him like he's a diapered papoose. His shell may be a bleached Bengal from the Himalayan foothills, but his mind is well advanced."

Shandao sat on a stump near the blazing bonfire. Turning toward Phoenix, the gaze in his cloudy eyes seemed to go back eons. "Why are you here?"

"I guess the same reason you're here: Emperia."

Shandao looked away dissatisfied, taking a deep breath.

Phoenix continued. "Well, your daughter is creating quite a fuss back home. We're wondering if you can help."

Shandao's silvery eyelashes rose, his beard quivered, looking back with fire in his eyes. "Why. Are. You. *Here...?*"

This time, the question was like a thunderclap and flash of lightning in the same instant: a direct hit. Phoenix knew he wasn't talking about any incidental *here*. He was talking about some culmination of chaos and divine order far beyond anywhere Phoenix's thoughts ever ventured. He finally shrugged his shoulders. "I don't know."

Shandao relaxed his face, eyes hinting of a smile. "*I don't know* is often the most honest answer a man can give."

After they stared into the fire for awhile, Shandao spoke. "So, why aren't you out chasing women instead of an old man and a strange leopard?"

"Chasing women? That's what got me here."

"You mean Morgan?" Shandao giggled. "What about chasing Himalaya? Was that just for fun, or was there a transcendent cause?"

"Truth is, I didn't really care about any of this. I just wanted my regular world back, until Mae explained what's at stake. Then, I realized..." He went silent.

"You realized what?" said Shandao, as if destiny hinged on his answer.

"I realized it's about more than me..."

In that moment of pure honesty, the hilt on Himalaya's harness began to pulsate with a clover-green glow.

This startled Shandao, who stared at the glowing hilt in confusion. "Himalaya, why is Ahna blinking?"

Shandao went over to grab the hilt and inspect it, but it flashed a white light and burned his fingers. "Ow! What's going on, Himalaya?"

The leopard, used to Shandao's antics, stood slowly, wittingly, and waltzed over to Phoenix.

Shandao stopped checking his fingers for blisters, and nodded at Phoenix. "*You*... Pick her up."

"Pick who up?"

"The sword."

"So I can get burned?"

"To see *if* she burns you."

Phoenix studied the golden hilt protruding from the black leather harness, the spiraling pattern on the hand grip glimmered in the firelight. He slid his forefinger along the metal, like testing a hot mug. Instead of getting burned, the hilt pulsated with an even brighter green light.

Shandao's eyes widened as Phoenix lifted the hilt and held it out before him. An emerald glowed where the hand grip met the cross-guard. Translucent and gleaming, the gem pulsated like a heartbeat.

Shandao approached, placing his hand on Phoenix's chest. "*Perfectly.*"

"Perfectly what?" said Phoenix.

"Beating to the rhythm of your heart."

19

Sparkling stars draped behind Phoenix like curtains of a stage. He stood between two mountain peaks, the sword firm in his grip.

Shandao watched from afar. "Say her name," he called out. "Ahna!"

Staring at the green gemstone on the hilt, Phoenix spoke with conviction. *"Ahna."* To his delight, a laser blade of smokeless fire sprang from the hilt.

He swung the sword back and forth, mesmerized by the trail of searing flames. He whirled it, watching the ring of fire around him. Increasing the speed, the flames formed a shield of blue fire.

Filled with a surge of confidence, Phoenix slashed into a chunk of granite. The blade sliced through the rock with a flashing sizzle, scattering ash to the wind.

"Go ahead and fire her," said Shandao. "Just like I lit the bonfire..."

Phoenix pulled the sword back like a catapult then thrusted it forward, launching a fiery orb from the sword's tip that struck a nearby boulder, bursting it to a puff of ash.

Days and nights passed as Phoenix learned new techniques under Shandao's guidance. The power of the sword captivated him, but he wondered why he was given such a weapon. Surely there'd be a price, some responsibility, to wield this wonder.

One evening on a mountaintop, after learning new

techniques, Phoenix looked over at Shandao. "It's like the sword is teaching me..." He walked to a cliff's edge and flipped the sword over his head, catching it with his other hand. As he whirled the sword in a figure eight pattern, picking up speed, the fiery trails formed wings at his sides.

For one flashing moment, Shandao beheld *The Phoenix.*

With newfound poise, Phoenix relaxed his stance, pressing the emerald on the hilt to retract the fiery blade.

Shandao resisted the urge to praise him, not wanting to inflate his ego, but he couldn't hide the glint of exuberance in his gaze.

They sat together on a rock, concerns of the future weighing on Shandao's thoughts as puzzles of the past filled Phoenix's mind.

"I've always wondered," said Phoenix. "What was Emperia like as a child?"

Shandao let the question absorb before answering clearly. "Clever as a fox. Fearless. Righteous."

Phoenix turned to him with sincerity. "So, just curious, why did you leave her?"

Shandao sighed, deciding if Phoenix was ready for the answer. Hearing the wind rattle branches of nearby pines, he knew he had to tell him. "She and I mastered the outside world, the parade of changing forms. But in the end, all the *stuff* disappears. Power shifts. Energy transfers. Even the sun and moon will eventually take on new forms. The only thing that lasts is what you cultivate within. Virtues attained through self-discipline extend beyond space and time. Selfless acts of loving kindness are like inner alchemy, turning us to gold within."

Phoenix took in the words for awhile before he spoke. "Have you always felt this way?"

"No..." Shandao's eyes glazed over in reflection. "My quest for wisdom began late in life. So, I missed the chance to help my daughter when she was young, when she would've listened more." He took a deep breath, cooling emotions still simmering, then spoke with vulnerability. "I was just another man caught in the illusion, fascinated by androids, with a daughter who wanted to turn women from victims to victors. Once we realized our wildest dreams, I watched helplessly while power corroded her heart like rust..."

Phoenix shook his head. "But it's not too late. Like you said, she's smart, brave, righteous."

Shandao smiled with fondness in his eyes, as if Phoenix just won him over. "Thats right, Phoenix. It's not too late. We can set her free, free of illusion, free of android control." He sighed. "She's afraid because she's not free."

20

Himalaya opened fire on Phoenix, shooting orbs of golden light from a gun on his harness. Phoenix blocked each shot with a swipe of his sword, swinging low and high. As the playful practice progressed, he noticed the sword burned brighter after absorbing each orb. "Ahna's feeding off your attacks!"

Raising the action a level, Himalaya fired two shots together. Phoenix blocked one but the other struck his calf. He fell onto the mountain stone, examining the red mark left behind, a mild burn. He sprang to his feet with grit in his grin. "Okay, make it a triple!"

Himalaya nodded and launched three orbs toward Phoenix at close intervals. He blocked the first two with a zig-zag motion of his sword and jumped the third.

Shandao stepped forward, nodding with a smile. "Well done, for now. Time for a new challenge, while the sun is strong." He looked at Phoenix. "So, city boy, ever climb a tree?"

"Ah, can't say I have."

"Even so, there's more information in your DNA about climbing trees than all the fodder you've been fed in the Fishbowl. Let's go find a suitable tree..."

They followed Shandao along a mountain trail to a forest.

"Himalaya, pick one you both can climb."

The muscular feline strolled along a line of trees, like a general inspecting soldiers. He approached a tropical cedar, magnificent in stature, its bark wrinkled like frozen waves.

"This is one of his favorites," said Shandao. "A napping haven, pleasant mix of sun and shade." Himalaya approached a giant palm tree stretching toward the stars. "That one's quite special too, overlooking a clearing where many a tasty morsel is known to pass. But unfortunately, no lower branches or vines to support a clawless biped." A giant Ceiba tree caught the leopard's attention, its light-colored trunk spread into the sky to support a canopy of dangling vines. "That one's just art. Words can't go there, just a pleasure to behold..."

"Will you guys just pick a tree?" said Phoenix.

Himalaya leapt onto the Ceiba and started crawling up the trunk with ease.

Shandao looked over at Phoenix. "Don't just stand there, follow him!"

Phoenix jumped onto the trunk, surprising himself as he scaled the organic tower, relying on twisting vines that thrived along the trunk.

He came to a lone vine dangling like a ladder to the higher branches, but it was out of reach. He stood upon a canopy of vines and jumped, but it was still too high.

"Look at the trunk!" Shandao spoke through the speaker on Himalaya's harness, watching below with binoculars.

Phoenix noticed a large knot bulging out of the trunk. He jumped onto the knot and immediately boosted himself off it to reach the vine. Pulling himself up the vine, he made it to the branches where he continued the climb with ease.

When he reached the branch just below Himalaya, he was about to join him, but the animal objected, shaking his furry head.

Phoenix realized it was for his own safety, as the branch may not support both of them. He relaxed and watched the shape-shifting clouds hover above the main island, hoping his friends weren't too worried about him. He planned to return to them soon.

After awhile, he looked up at Himalaya. "First one down wins!"

Himalaya didn't like the idea, shaking his head adamantly.

"See ya!" Phoenix said as he leapt to a lower branch, then dropped onto the next branch.

Himalaya took care as he maneuvered down the tree, displeased by Phoenix's race to the bottom.

"Going down is more dangerous than climbing up!" hollered Shandao from the ground. "Slow down!"

Phoenix continued his rapid descent, glancing up at times to check on Himalaya's progress. As he made it to the lowest and oldest branch above the canopy of vines, a quiet voice within him suggested he ease down gently. But his ego was set on winning. He heard leaves quiver above as Himalaya drew closer. Phoenix took a bold leap, but the branch couldn't hold the impact, so it snapped.

Phoenix free-fell, ripping through the canopy of vines toward a granite landing...

A thud against his back was the last thing Phoenix felt. From then on, visuals had brilliant, iridescent edges. Mountains and trees seemed painted with strokes of light. He floated out of his body and was somehow able to look down at Shandao checking the pulse on his neck and slapping his chest.

Despite the scene, Phoenix felt utter peace. He traveled up through a glowing portal of shimmering light. Tranquility saturated his being as he beheld a radiance like the sun. He could barely make out his mother's face, just as she appeared before her untimely death, holding an image of Christ with sun rays beaming from his chest, casting an aura of loving kindness.

It was then Phoenix fully understood the concept of telepathy, for there were no words, just a message that animated his imagination. *There's more to do...* A light flashed, so blinding that Phoenix was forced to turn away.

Looking down to the ground, he saw Shandao frantically searching the various pockets of Himalaya's harness. "He needs a good jolt!"

Phoenix had to laugh as he felt the air in his lungs again. Despite an aching backside, he was filled with gratitude.

"There we go!" gasped Shandao. "I thought we lost you!"

Phoenix sat up, feeling profound mental clarity, a sense of peace pervading the air around him.

"Something's different about you," said Shandao, staring into Phoenix's serene eyes.

After Phoenix described his mystical experience, Shandao sat back on a bed of moss. "I've come to know one thing in my later years. We're here to fulfill a destiny, whether we realize it or not. We have guides along the way who bring truth, light and love; reminding us that our bodies each carry an eternal Soul. Nobody can take that away, but too much focus on the mind's illusions makes us forget it."

Compassion softened Shandao's weathered features. "On your journey, remember this vision. Contemplate on it often. You can experience this pure light without having to nearly die first."

Silence followed, a sweet kind Phoenix savored. He envisioned the transcendental light, the aura of peace. Then, like Bandhu instructed, he watched his breath. After awhile, he merged the two, meditating on a brilliant orb of light rising and falling with each breath. He began to feel a glow in his heart region. The light he saw outside his body was now like a spark within him. He sensed it was always there, but now he was becoming aware of it.

Just as the state of peace seemed unbreakable, Shandao stood swiftly and spoke. "Looks like we have an unexpected visitor..."

Phoenix opened his eyes to see a CloudRunner ominously approaching in the distance. He lifted Shandao's binoculars from the ground and gazed through them, recognizing the driver in the garb of an Emperial Guard, curly dark hair flying in the wind, chin and cheeks raised. Rudeen had found them.

Astonished, Phoenix stood. "That's my Role Officer."

"She followed you here?" said Shandao, alarmed.

"Rudeen!" he called out, but the craft was already well on its way to the main island. Phoenix knew an Emperial CloudRunner wouldn't be welcomed by Rhain's people. Concerned for her safety, he charged out of the canyon, heading toward the cave that led to the waterfall entrance.

"Phoenix, there's more you need to know!" But he just kept running. "Be good to Ahna," Shandao said with a sigh, knowing Phoenix was already gone.

21

The orange sub took Phoenix back to the main island where a crowd gathered on the shore. They jeered and shouted at Rudeen as she circled above in the CloudRunner.

Mae ran down the beach to greet Phoenix. "We've been looking everywhere for you!"

"I found Shandao."

She beamed. "That was my hope."

Azalea ran up to Phoenix and swept him into a hug. "We missed you, Fee. We worried that big cat ate ya'!"

Lars arrived, grinning at the sight of their comrade, giving him a fist-bump. But the celebration didn't last long, as some of the warrior men stomped toward them.

A woman ran up to Mae, pointing skyward at the CloudRunner. "That craft is from Emperia! You brought her here, endangering our home." Tears welled in her eyes.

Another man chimed in. "She will destroy the whole island when she finds you here."

Down the beach, Halzac emerged from the brush with the BoltRifle on his shoulder. Taking aim at the CloudRunner, he struck the craft's HoverJets with a flashing bolt.

Rudeen ejected, parachute flying, as the CloudRunner splashed into the ocean and bobbed like an electrified buoy.

As the people erupted in cheers, Halzac took a bow.

"What are you doing?" Phoenix yelled. "That's Rudeen!"

"How was I supposed to know!" said Halzac. "Besides, I

only took out the jets."

Phoenix jumped in the water and swam toward Rudeen as the parachute carried her into the ocean.

As men sped by Phoenix in canoes, he grabbed the stern of one to let it tug him. Rudeen's life jacket kept her afloat as she called out, "I bring you urgent news!" But when they reached her, two of the warriors raised their spears. Rudeen drew her lasergun. "Stay back!"

"Stop, everyone!" yelled Phoenix. "Rudeen, put the gun down. It's okay."

Before she could make another move, Rudeen was tugged underwater. Phoenix swam down to see a man holding her under while another twisted the lasergun from her hand. When they emerged, two other men pulled her into the canoe and bound her hands with rope.

When Phoenix made it back to the shore, he found Rudeen tied to a palm tree, winded and dazed. He approached the men and women around her. "Please ... release her."

A woman took the lasergun from the warrior and examined it. "She uses a weapon from the Electric Queen, wears her fashions, flies her craft." The woman raised the gun to strike Rudeen with the grip, but Azalea snatched her off the ground before she swung. Mae pulled the gun from the woman's hand as Azalea set her back down.

The warriors rushed in, spears in motion, violence flaring in their eyes.

Phoenix drew his sword. "Ahna!" Flames burst forth. Everyone beheld the strange blade of smokeless flame.

Rhain rushed onto the scene. "What's happening here? Phoenix, put that away!"

Phoenix powered down Ahna and walked over to Rudeen.

"This is our friend, Rudeen. Please ask them to release her."

Rhain looked at Rudeen's sopping wet Emperial Guard uniform. "How can this be?"

"She helped us beat the GameBots, gave me a code word that froze them so we could score the last points."

Rhain took out a knife and sliced through the rope to unbind her.

Lars stepped out of the crowd and offered her a split coconut.

"Thank you." Rudeen drank the milk ravenously, then took a deep breath, looking at Mae and Phoenix. "I've come to warn you. Emperia tracked an unidentified submarine to this island."

Mae stepped forward. "How long do we have?"

"I'm afraid the warships aren't far behind me..."

"Warships?" said Azalea.

"Yeah, three of 'em..." said Halzac, pointing to the ocean. Everyone turned to see three distant ships on the horizon.

Rhain raised her arms. "Everyone, to the shelter!" One man took out a bull-roarer, like a small surf board connected to rawhide string, and whirled it furiously. A deep whistle howled out, quickly replicated across the island.

22

Dusk fell as Emperial warships loomed offshore. Halzac crouched behind a boulder, gazing through the scope of the BoltRifle to survey the decks filled with cannons and missile launchers.

Then, all in an instant, smoke and flashing lights erupted from the three ships. Halzac ducked behind the boulder as missiles tore through the atmosphere. But instead of spreading hellfire and terror, the missiles exploded in a dazzling display of fireworks. Red, white and blue lights bloomed in the evening sky.

Halzac stood up, mustache crooked with an ironic smile.

As the lights burned out, the battleships beamed a giant hologram into the smoke. Emperia's sullen, white face filled the evening sky, heart-shaped lips painted cherry red. "Inhabitants of this island, I come in peace."

Halzac laughed. "And I'm a walrus."

"I have one demand. Turn over Miss O'Herra to me. There's much I need to discuss with her after she left in such a tizzy. I expect immediate compliance, unless you'd like to face the fury of a woman scorned."

A male announcer spoke as the hologram of Emperia faded to black. "We'll be right back with live coverage of Operation Dis-Mae following a word from your friendly neighborhood WaitBot."

An image of a WaitBot filled the smoky air, holding a tray

as he stood in a black suit and silver tie. He spoke with a voice similar to Vincent's, but deeper. "How may I make your day amazing, Madam?"

A female announcer spoke. "Behind every successful woman is a robot. Today's androids can do everything a woman-on-the-go could ask for, like loading the dishes, scrubbing floors, weeding the garden and so much more!" Scenes showed the bot performing each job, finishing with a close-up of his gleaming, smiling face. "Androids, a woman's best friend."

The hologram showed Earth spinning below the outline of an eye with a lowercase "e" in the center. A female voice spoke cryptically. "*Over land, sea, and air: Emperia is everywhere.*"

The announcer resumed speaking. "We return live from the Caribbean Sea for a major turning point in Operation Dis-Mae... It appears Mae is turning herself in!"

"What? No she's not," said Halzac as the beach lit up from the warships' spotlights. There stood Mae, illuminated, arms spread, wearing a white gown that flowed in the wind. A live hologram of her image filled the sky: eyes closed, standing tall, a willing sacrifice.

Three HoverCopters painted in camouflage launched from the closest battleship. The streamlined crafts sailed over the dark waters toward her.

"This ain't happenin'!" Halzac yelled, charging for the shore with his BoltRifle.

Two copters landed beside Mae while a third one hovered above her. She remained poised as two cables fell from the copter and grappled her arms, pulling her up swiftly into the cabin of the craft.

"*Why*, Mae?" Halzac said as he took cover behind a

boulder. He raised his rifle and fixed the sight on the HoverCopter returning to the ship with Mae. He knew he couldn't shoot, so he aimed at one of the copters still on the sand. He pulled the trigger and a flashing bolt struck the craft, enveloping it in a web of electricity. Two Embots jumped out with laser rifles drawn. Halzac opened fire, taking them both out with rapid-fire blasts of controlled lightning.

The two remaining HoverCopters activated blue energy shields. One raised a bulb-like device from its roof and saturated the area with a blinding flash. The wave of energy made Halzac's rifle crackle and short-circuit. He dropped it like a hot coal.

Two more Embots marched out of the other copter. Halzac retreated, ducking behind the boulder. The bots' eyes shot bright beams to scan the area, stopping on the boulder near Halzac. They launched an assault with their laser rifles, reducing the boulder to rubble.

Halzac sprinted into the forest, hearing their feet pound the ground behind him. He tore through the forest, searching for a hole to jump in, a tree to climb, anywhere to hide.

One of the Embots stopped and opened fire, hitting shrubs right next to him. The burst threw him against a palm tree. He fell, out of wind, as the bot closed in on him.

Not the type to panic, Halzac calmly stared down the barrel of the bot's rifle. "Do I at least get a last cigar?"

Before the Embot pulled the trigger, a fireball flew over Halzac and struck the bot square in the eyes. With a popping flash, the android collapsed. Halzac looked back to see Phoenix wielding his newfound wonder, Ahna.

The other Embot fired back at Phoenix, who whirled his sword to catch and absorb the blast. He returned fire with a strike that made night seem like day again.

"Woohoo!" yelled Halzac, all bots now sizzling. He watched the two empty HoverCopters return to the battleships on autopilot, one flying lopsided from the BoltRifle's sting.

23

Watching the warships depart with Mae, Phoenix stood motionless. Rudeen appeared behind him, placing her hand on his shoulder, feeling his tenseness. "We'll find a way to help Mae. All is not lost."

Before he could reply, the base of the departing battleships began to glow, exposing the inner sea life like an x-ray. Coral, seaweed and fish became visible, a splendid scene at first, until the fish scurried for their lives and the top of the sea began to boil.

Rudeen tugged Phoenix's arm. "We should get to the shelter like everyone else."

Phoenix watched lasers launch into the clouds from the ships' towering masts. "She's so unpredictable..." The lasers connected in a vortex where dark clouds materialized. As the ships continued moving away from the island, the massive clouds grew, swirling faster and faster. The vortex pulled in surrounding clouds as it swelled into a massive storm.

"There's nothing we can do now," said Rudeen. "If anything, Mae needs us alive more than ever."

The wind howled, spraying seawater as tree branches swayed violently. Rudeen grabbed Phoenix's hand, tugging him along toward the shelter. But the landscape transformed in the chaos of the synthetic storm. Falling debris covered paths.

Sandy gusts blinded them.

Rudeen shouted above the fury, "I can't see the path!"

Palm trees arched toward the ground and sea waters raged as they searched for any sign of the path to the shelter.

Finally, at the base of a hill, Phoenix saw a blue light flashing. He led Rudeen up the hill where they discovered a small opening to a cave. Crouching down, they walked through a tunnel which grew larger as they reached a wooden door. They entered a cavern furnished with a large, round table and primitive wooden chairs.

On the table was the source of the blue light: a muscular four-legged beast with fierce eyes and a collar holding a glowing blue jewel.

Rudeen gasped, but Phoenix recognized the hefty feline. "Himalaya," he said with a smile.

"What, you tamed him too?"

Phoenix shook his head. "He arrived with Shandao."

"Himalaya cast a beam from his harness to light a nearby wood oven, quickly warming the damp chamber. Smoke flowed up a stone chimney.

Rudeen admired the mysterious snow leopard in all his glory, finding his glistening gray eyes kind and protective.

"You're magnificent," she said. "Thanks for saving us." She turned to Phoenix with a laugh, then punched him in the shoulder. "I was really about to freak out there."

As they took in the soothing heat of the fire, she looked over at him, green eyes gleaming. He held his breath waiting for her to speak, as if back in the Fishbowl.

"Relax," she said, shaking her head. "I'm not your Role Officer anymore."

He smiled. "When I first met you, I thought you were quite

the bad-ass. I was pretty much petrified of you."

She nodded. "That's how we want it."

"But over time, I realized you were really on my side."

"It took you long enough."

He noticed the golden chain around her neck with a pendant tucked into her breastplate. He gently slid his finger along the chain to reveal a perfectly round pearl. Staring into the gem, he saw his reflection in the polished sheen.

An indigo light glowed from Himalaya's harness, followed by a chime. Phoenix looked over. "What is it, Himalaya?"

As the leopard opened his eyes, the voice of Shandao crackled through a speaker on his harness. "Phoenix, are you there?" Amid the raging wind and rain, his voice was barely audible. "Can you hear me?"

Phoenix jumped to his feet. "Yes! We're safe, Shandao. Where are you? Sounds like you're caught in the storm."

"I am." There was a long pause as the rain pelted. "In essence, I helped create this storm. Tonight, I will no longer run from my karma. I'm facing what's mine. If this is the hour I am destined to leave the Earth, my work will continue on the other side. I no longer doubt that."

Himalaya stood erect and growled in protest. "Now, now, Himalaya," said Shandao. "You must trust. There are many dimensions... They're all connected."

"We lost Mae," said Phoenix.

"No, we haven't. She eventually had to confront Emperia. The time has arrived." Thunder rumbled. "Remember that light within you, Phoenix, resonating from your heart. It not only connects you to Ahna, but to the higher power behind the changing forms." The rain swished through the speaker. "Himalaya, take care of Phoenix."

Himalaya's growl shrank to the yowl of bitter acceptance. The last noise through the speaker was a thud and the whipping of wet wind.

24

The legendary builder of Emperial robots stood atop a cliff by an ancient tree. Wind ripped into the coast. He bowed with eyes closed, stepping apart from the protective tree to face the storm. The threads in his robe stretched back to show the knobby bones that forged the Age of Androids. He looked into the heavens, hands folded as if asking for mercy, while at the same time emptying himself to receive a grace beyond understanding.

The whirling tempest whipped the island like a beast, howling with a wild, ominous fury. A fierce gust made Shandao lose his footing. As he was blown back against the elder tree, a mighty branch cracked and collapsed on him. He breathed his last breath looking skyward, mangled limbs blending with the tree's exposed root system, blood bringing the tree new life, spirit set free.

25

Emperia stood atop the battleship balcony wearing a navy blue overcoat embroidered with silver clouds. She gazed into the midnight ocean, purple-black with unlimited potential. Lightning crackled above the two islands from the storm of her making.

And then the hammer fell, the weight of the spirit crushing the mind. She fell to her knees, her body like iron as she collapsed. The bones in her hands pounded onto the damp planks. She could smell the wood. Space and time spiraled into a void. Using all her strength, she tried to remain conscious.

Vincent appeared, shiny metallic in the cool night air, face full of manufactured concern. He crouched by her. "What is it, Madam President?" He waved his hand over her, scanning her vitals.

"He was there," gasped Emperia. "On the island."

"Who are you referring to, Madam President?"

"Father... My father has passed." She began to shiver.

"I have no data to indicate Shandao was killed. I monitor every known network, even networks he thinks are secure."

"There's a network you can't reach..."

"I'm sorry Madam President. I don't understand."

She looked up at Vincent. Emptiness filled her. Out of the whole world, there was only a machine there to comfort her, mimicking emotion without fully grasping the mysteries of life and death.

26

Phoenix sat near the wood-fired oven, watching his breath, visualizing the light he saw after his fall. He felt a warmth in his chest as Ahna's emerald glowed brighter, pulsating to the rhythm of his heart.

Himalaya curled up in a corner of the cavern, missing his master. Phoenix also mourned the loss of Shandao, but something within him sensed his presence still lingering.

Rudeen paced nervously as the sound of flowing water grew louder outside their chamber. "Phoenix, I think the cave is starting to flood!"

Phoenix and Himalaya both rose as a gush of floodwater slammed the entry door shut, sealing it with the force of water and loose rocks.

Rudeen pushed the door, but it wouldn't budge.

Water streamed through the opening at the base of the door. Luckily, natural cracks in the stone floor let most of the floodwater drain.

After the storm waters subsided, they settled into a slumber on top of the table.

Dawn arrived, undetectable in their sealed quarters. Himalaya poked Phoenix's chin with his nose. Phoenix woke to see a flashing red light on the leopard's harness. A screen reported, "Oxygen low."

With water and stone still blocking the doorway, Phoenix knew he couldn't just slash open the door with his sword, or the cavern could quickly flood.

Himalaya activated a flashlight and they searched for another exit.

As the temperature inside the cave soared, Rudeen awoke, brow sweating. "It's so hot..."

"Hey there," said Phoenix. "We're finding a way out."

Himalaya scanned the cave ceiling, stopping on a circular tile near the top that had a carving of the sun etched into it.

"Could be a portal for sunlight," said Phoenix.

Rudeen sighed. "But so high..."

Phoenix lifted the hilt from the golden sheath on his belt. "*Ahna.*" The fiery blade sprang forth and he lunged the sword forward, launching a fireball that burst the tile to pieces. Loose rocks streamed out of the opening, filling the cavern with dust, making everyone cough.

Then, triumphantly, a rope ladder fell from the opening.

"Well, would you look at that," said Rudeen.

Phoenix put away Ahna and ascended the ladder through the blackened portal. When he reached the top, he pushed open a trapdoor, unveiling a crystalline blue sky. The precious air never smelled so sweet.

Crawling out, he found himself on a tiled platform at the side of a mountain. He beheld a most unexpected sight: near a marble alter, incense burned from a bronze thurible as a small crowd gathered. Rhain approached, wearing a black and gold ceremonial tunic, disbelief freezing her tongue. Warriors surrounded Phoenix, staring at him like a ghost.

"Hallelujah!" yelled Azalea, running through the crowd and hugging him.

Lars appeared, then Halzac. "Welcome to your funeral."

"My funeral?"

Rhain stepped forward. "Indeed, The Phoenix rises."

Phoenix looked down the tunnel. "All clear!"

After Rudeen emerged, Himalaya appeared behind her, grappling the rungs of the ladder with his powerful paws. The crowd went quiet as some of the warriors raised spears.

Phoenix petted the big cat. "This is Himalaya, a trained snow leopard."

Several of the youths were the first to approach and pet the elusive creature. As Himalaya sat down to enjoy the free massage, weapons were relaxed. Soon, people of all ages gathered around to admire the gentle leopard.

Phoenix looked out from the mountainside, seeing the fallen trees and wind-whipped crops. Knowing the arrival of Team Human led to the chaos, his heart grew heavy.

Hearing a rumbling of voices on the shore, Phoenix noticed warriors surrounding their lifeboat. They pulled the boat out of the sand and hurled it into the ocean, like throwing a stowaway overboard.

The warriors turned and approached the mountainside. One pointed at Phoenix and his friends. "If they aren't gone by sundown, we'll remove them by force."

Another called out. "And we want the fire sword! That is the least they owe us."

"Well, you ain't getting it!" hollered Halzac.

Phoenix also knew he couldn't just give away Ahna, and he didn't want to fight about it. As Halzac and the warrior argued, he removed the sheath holding the sword and re-attached it to Himalaya's harness, where he first found it. "Go, Himalaya. Take Ahna to safety," he whispered. "I'll be near the boat at sundown."

Himalaya slipped into the brush and disappeared along the

back of the mountain. He made it all the way to the shore near the sandbar and vanished in the ocean.

Phoenix stepped forward to address the warriors. "The sword is gone."

"The leopard took it!" a woman yelled.

The warrior didn't know how to respond, except to scowl fiercely and grip his spear.

"That sword is not for us," said Rhain. "Nature provides everything we need. We must not crave such devices. Our way is simple. Our path is true. Let that be the end of it."

Team Human walked somberly down the mountain and spent the afternoon cleaning the lifeboat and checking for infirmities. The open-air vessel, fit for six, featured a carbon fiber hull that was light yet strong. However, the engine was destroyed, deliberately dismantled, leaving them only sails and paddles.

Rudeen popped open a cabinet and pulled out one of the sails. "It's been awhile, but I think I remember enough..." She and Phoenix spent another hour securing the sails before hoisting them.

As the sun met the horizon, Phoenix grew nervous. "I haven't seen Himalaya..."

Rudeen scanned the area. "He knows we're here. Probably keeping a low profile." She nodded toward a group of warriors at the edge of the forest, weapons and painted faces on display.

"Himalaya!" Phoenix yelled in every direction. He looked toward the sandbar where he once followed the feline into the murky depths.

Walking down to the shore, he let the waves roll over his feet. While he looked around, a large wave struck his shins. Then, a larger one wet his knees as the wind increased. Phoenix thought he heard a whisper meshing with the waves. *"Let him find you."*

"Shandao?"

Another wave rolled in and he heard the voice again but more clearly. *"Go. Trust."*

Phoenix's mouth fell open, startled.

Rudeen appeared behind him. "Who are you talking to?"

Phoenix repeated the whisper. "Go. Trust..."

She smiled at him quizzically, then turned toward the evening sun above the vast ocean. "Time to take to the sea." They walked back to the boat where the rest of Team Human gathered.

A thin, darkly tanned man appeared with a wide-brimmed leather hat, holding several clay jugs. "I'm Tonku, the shaman." He gave one jug to Phoenix. "This one is for sustenance, if you run out of food." He gave one to Rudeen. "This is medicine, if you get seasick." He handed the last one to Halzac. "And this is rum, if you get sick of each other." He winked.

"Tonku, I see you're a man of many wonders!" said Halzac.

The shaman gave Rhain a scroll. "They will need the star chart."

"Thank you, Tonku," said Rhain. "Your help is invaluable."

Halzac wasn't impressed. "We're supposed to replace our navigation system with a crinkled up map?"

"What he's trying to say is," said Phoenix. "We're used to computers telling us where to go. We may need help with the chart."

"That's why I'm joining you," said Rhain.

Everyone turned toward Rhain in surprise, but Tonku was the most shocked. "You're needed here to guide our daily affairs."

"I will return, but I must help them reach their destination. The Electric Queen attacked our island, and she's broken our peace before. The least I can do is help her adversaries, our friends."

"I understand," said Tonku. "We shall have to accept."

"Tonku, I appoint you to guide our people during my absence."

"I will do my best."

"So, where are you taking us?" said Phoenix.

"We'll first stop at Agoura. It's a small island that will give us a chance to rest and replenish. After that, it's up to you where we go."

"America," said Halzac. "East Coast."

"Then that's where we'll go."

"In this dinky thing?" said Azalea. "Y'all gonna drive me batshit crazy on the open seas!"

Halzac scoffed. "We love you too."

"Don't worry, my friends," said Rhain. "I'll get you to your destination safely. This vessel will more than suffice."

Phoenix smiled. "I've read about men sailing thousands of miles in boats more primitive than this, with just the wind and paddles."

Azalea shook her head. "Tonku, we're gonna need a lot more of that rum!"

27

The shore shrank as the moon broke through rolling clouds. Wind filled the sails, pushing Team Human into the vast unknown.

Phoenix found himself at peace amid the expansive freedom of the sea, but he could tell others were nervous. "Remember when we trusted Mae to lead us anywhere and we'd go? Well, now it's time to trust each other."

Rhain smiled. "Well said. Trust is key."

"I trust everyone here," said Halzac. "With one possible exception." He tilted his head toward Rudeen.

Azalea laughed. "He just called you out, girl."

"I don't blame you," said Rudeen. "Here I am dressed like an Emperial Guard ... and I was a Role Officer for years."

"Certified ball buster," said Halzac.

Azalea giggled. "Nailed it."

Rudeen turned melancholic. "I realize nobody has any reason to trust me."

"Yes, we do," said Phoenix. "You helped us win the game."

"That's true," said Azalea, stroking her chin.

"Either way, I guess we're stuck with each other," Halzac said with a sigh, then leaned back and closed his eyes.

The cool nocturnal air pacified the crew. Soon, most drifted into a blissful sleep, riding waves of oceanic dreamscape.

Rhain and Phoenix stayed awake, analyzing the sky against the chart of stars. As Phoenix tried to make sense of it all, he noticed Rudeen clenching her fists in her sleep. Sweat formed on her brow as she mumbled incoherently. He assumed she was having a nightmare and hoped it would subside.

Then suddenly, she awoke with a possessed gaze, shaking as if frigid. "I, I need a Scrip... Does anyone have a VaporScrip? So cold..."

Phoenix grabbed another blanket and wrapped it around her, but she kept shivering. When he leaned against her to bring her heat, she reacted violently. "Get off me!"

Halzac awoke and saw her eyes and pale color. "Withdrawal. There's nothing you can do but ride it out, babe."

She hissed. "Don't call me babe!"

Azalea looked at Rhain. "Maybe a taste of rum would help?"

Rudeen gasped. "Gimme it!" Halzac reached into a cabinet and pulled out the jug of rum. When he gave it to her, she ripped off the cork and started guzzling.

"Rudeen!" Phoenix yelled but she kept drinking. Finally, he grabbed the jug from her, spilling some onto the boat.

Rudeen lunged at him, but Azalea held her back in a bear hug. "Easy, girl!"

"Men would take away everything again!" she yelled at Phoenix. "Emperia *knows* how you are!"

Her words stung. Phoenix felt like he was in the Fishbowl again, but worse.

"Her reason is gone," said Rhain.

"How many Scrips were you takin', sister?" said Azalea, letting her go.

"None of your business!" Rudeen began coughing savagely,

sweating even more profusely.

She leaned over the side of the boat, projecting rum and stomach acid into the ocean. Phoenix cringed at the sour smell. Her head hung overboard for awhile, then she collapsed and curled into a fetal position. The shivering now came in waves.

Phoenix laid blankets over her. She began humming sorrowfully as the shaking eased. It was a sad, lonely tune through trembling lips. After some time, Phoenix offered her some water and she sipped it. Just before dawn, she grabbed him and pulled him close. "I didn't mean it."

"I know," said Phoenix, and they both fell into a deep sleep.

The morning's first rays lit the sea, the clouds, and Phoenix's consciousness. He checked on Rudeen, grateful to see her sleeping soundly.

"Take the wheel," Rhain said to Phoenix. "I'll rest now. Just sail with the sun at your back." She lay down in a cozy nook and closed her eyes.

Soon, Lars, Azalea and Halzac greeted the day. Rudeen was the last to wake. Sitting up slowly, she covered her eyes. "So bright..." When she looked out again at the endless ocean, she became apprehensive. "Are we lost?"

"No worries," said Phoenix. "We're on our way to a small island, a rest stop."

Rudeen joined Phoenix behind the wheel of the ship, fitting on the same chair. He adjusted the wheel to turn the rudder as fresh wind filled the sails, carrying the boat swiftly. "Rhain will like our progress," said Phoenix. After some sailing, the winds grew to gusts as dark clouds rolled toward them. "So much for our sunny day..."

The first drops woke Rhain, who went to adjust the sails. The growing wind first sounded like a fan, then rose to the roar of a turbine engine. Rain pellets felt like needles as the crew had no choice but to sail into a wall of water.

"Grab the buckets!" yelled Rhain. "Lars and Azalea, stay at the oars and keep pulling!" Phoenix and Halzac bailed water furiously to keep the boat from sinking.

"Faster!" shouted Rudeen as she and Rhain held onto the sails to keep them steady. The waves were now like mountains of molten iron rising and falling.

As the flooded ship swayed back and forth, the ship tilted over so far that cargo spilled from the open cabinets. A powerful gust flipped the sail around, striking Rhain and ripping. "Keep bailing!" she said, ignoring the blow to her head. The next forty minutes felt like forty days as everyone worked incessantly to keep the boat from succumbing to the storm, bailing water almost as fast as the clouds dropped it.

Just as it looked like they were becoming one with the sea, the head of the storm passed, leaving behind a light shower. But any sense of relief was eclipsed by the realization that most of their food and supplies were lost in the storm. "No! Not the rum too!" said Halzac as he searched for the jug.

"Hate to break the bad news," said Rhain. "But we have no food, no medicine, no fishing gear..."

"And no rum," said Halzac.

"Quit with your rum!" said Azalea. "Who do you think left the cabinets open?"

Halzac's face filled with a mix of guilt and anger.

"Let's not look back," said Phoenix. "At least we're alive."

Rhain nodded. "We can still make it to the island, to eat, rest and repair the sail." She slid her hand along one of the many rips.

Azalea sighed. "This island better show up soon..."

The showers subsided as the evening clouds covered them like a blanket. Phoenix and his cohorts were tired, hungry and downtrodden. While most of them dreamt of a variety of foods, Halzac dreamt of rum.

At dawn came serenity. But without any wind, they had to take turns paddling under a blazing sun. The day passed mostly in silence, all hoping for at least a breeze to boost them to the island.

But they would never reach the island.

During the magic hour between light and dark, amid utter stillness, the boat began to sway... Then, the sea bubbled and swirled below them, throwing the vessel to and fro. Finally, the boat keeled over, tossing everyone overboard.

"I can't swim!" screamed Azalea. Lars pulled her close, helping her hang on to the capsized boat.

"Emperia, I know this is you!" Halzac yelled at the sky, treading water. "She's probably broadcasting *this* live."

While they struggled to stay afloat, a glow appeared in the sea below them. Phoenix watched multicolored lights coming closer until they stood on the curved surface of a mammoth ship rising from the ocean.

As the vessel lifted them out of the water, Phoenix looked down at the colorful plates of the craft. He recognized the elegant tortoise-inspired design. "Oliver..."

"Bless my soul," said Azalea. "Ollie's gonna take us home."

28

A plate on Oliver's shell opened and an elevated platform took Team Human to the sub's lobby. They were greeted by a feast already prepared on a banquet table.

Azalea ran over to survey the spread. "Roast turkey and tart-cherry dressing, mashed potatoes and gravy, biscuits and honey, *honey*!"

Rudeen went to the bar area and returned with a tray filled with glasses of white wine. "To Team Human!" They toasted and drank down the sweet wine.

Rhain raised her arms for a blessing. "Thank you, Creator. Thank you, my brothers and sisters. And thank you, turkey!"

Halzac cut everyone a slice and they feasted in delight. After all were full and content, Phoenix looked around, "So, where's the Doctor?"

"Yeah," said Azalea. "Where is that lovely man? I want to thank him!"

"I look forward to meeting him," said Rhain, resting her head on her arm and closing her eyes. Within moments, she was sound asleep.

Azalea chuckled. "She ate herself to sleep."

Halzac also fell into a slumber, rolling his head back and snoring gently.

"Now, y'all makin' *me* sleepy," said Azalea, rubbing her eyes and resting her head on Lars' shoulder. He leaned back on her, and they fell asleep together.

Phoenix looked over at Rudeen, the only other one still awake. "Are you tired?"

Rudeen just stared at him as a tear seeped from the corner of her eye.

"What's wrong, Rudeen? What's happening here?"

Two doors slid open at opposite walls. Like a nightmare, two Embots emerged with laser rifles drawn.

Someone appeared behind the bar. Shiny-black armor hugged her toned body. Her silky brown hair, fierce cheek bones and glistening hazel eyes transported Phoenix back to the night he first followed Morgan. Now, there was no doubt she survived her leap from the roof. And with Embots at her side, there was no doubt Emperia sent her.

Phoenix approached her. "Where's the Doctor? Morgan, what have you done?"

She smiled mischievously and threw ice cubes into some tumblers, adding vodka and bubbling tonic with a twist of lime. "Have another drink. You're gonna need it." She looked over at Rudeen. "I've got one for you too, Rudy ... a reward for their capture."

Phoenix stared at Rudeen with a mix of disbelief and hurt.

Rudeen dropped her head as Morgan marched over to her.

"A Role Officer should never fall for one of her fellows."

"I'm fine!" Rudeen said, looking up with tears that betrayed her words.

"Hand over the tracking device," Morgan said. Rudeen removed her gold necklace that held the pearly sphere and gave it to Morgan.

Phoenix felt scorched, like his heart melted into lava and filled his stomach.

Rudeen got up to leave, but as she walked past the Embots,

Morgan stopped her. "Wait! Bind him." Morgan handed Rudeen a small square box. "Or I will report your emotional attachment to this felon. Trusted Role Officers don't cry when capturing a stray."

Rudeen glared at Morgan with disdain. She turned to face Phoenix, voice quivering. "Hands behind your back, please."

Morgan sneered. "Please? Dominate him!"

Rudeen met his gaze, unable to bring herself to bind him and complete the betrayal.

"This is ridiculous," Morgan yelled. "Bots, knock him down!" One of the Embots threw Phoenix to the floor, pressing his face against the tiles with its bony hand. The other Embot held his arms behind his back. "Now, Rudeen, restrain him like the fugitive he is!"

Rudeen gulped, like swallowing a bitter pill, as she leaned down by Phoenix and pushed the button on the box. Two cords sprang out and wrapped around his wrists like steel snakes.

Morgan turned to one of the Embots. "Escort Rudeen to her cabin." The bot led Rudeen out of the room. "And get over it!" cracked Morgan. "You have your Scrips again. Go inhale a few … dozen!" Morgan cackled as Rudeen followed the Embot out of the lobby.

The bots pulled Phoenix to his feet. Morgan sauntered over to him with her seductive yet destructive air. "Unlike your friends, you might go places. Emperia has plans for you. I hope you're ready."

She circled Phoenix like a predator sizing up wounded prey. "This is a pivotal moment for you, Phoenix. You can evolve from victim of circumstance to master of destiny."

Phoenix stood strong, despite his bound hands. "Why didn't you drug me too?"

Morgan leaned into his face and whispered with intensity. "If you can overcome your misplaced affection toward your Role Officer and repent your crimes against Emperia, doors of opportunity could open."

"Liberty or death," uttered Phoenix.

"You're on the wrong side of reality. Your motto should be, Emperia or death."

Morgan and an Embot escorted Phoenix down a long corridor to the ship's bridge.

Doctor Bandhu sat in the captain's chair with a pair of Embots watching him. Phoenix noticed the Doctor looked roughed up, hair mangled, a dried streak of blood coming from his lip.

"Activate the communications system," said Morgan.

"I will not," said Bandhu.

"I can easily hack into this ship's operating system. I'm tired of playing with you."

Phoenix looked up at an intercom in the ceiling. "Oliver! Where are you?" But there was no response, just an eerie silence.

"He's with us, Phoenix," said Bandhu. "Just waiting for the right moment."

"Oliver, is it?" said Morgan as she walked over to Bandhu. "Turn over full control of Oliver to me immediately."

Bandhu stood from the chair, looked up at the ceiling and yelled, "Oliver, no matter what happens to me, do everything in your power to eject these intruders and assist Phoenix and his team."

"That's it," said Morgan. She drew her lasergun and blasted Bandhu in the chest, leaving a charred hole in his white coat as he staggered backward. Phoenix lunged toward Morgan but an

Embot yanked back on the SnakeCuffs binding him.

Bandhu fell to the floor, looking at Phoenix. "May you ... achieve your destiny." And with that, he collapsed.

Morgan scanned his body with her ring. "His life force is strong. His heart still beats." She aimed her lasergun at him again, but stopped short of pulling the trigger, turning to the Embots. "Dispose of him into the sea, alive." The bots grabbed his arms and legs and carried him off the bridge. "The sharks will like his warm blood."

Phoenix couldn't believe this was the same woman he first found so alluring. "Who or *what* are you?"

"It's time you know. I am the fulfillment of Emperia's ultimate vision: the world's first Fembot."

"What?" Phoenix shook his head, even as it started to make sense. "Halzac said this Fembot was to do Emperia's dirty work... Is that what you are, a heartless automaton?"

A proud smile swept across Morgan's face. "That's right. I'm no bag of blood, bones and mixed feelings. I have one primary directive: to serve the One and Only Emperia."

She approached the captain's chair and grappled the controls on the arm. As electricity flowed from her hand into the chair, a hologram appeared of a LifeRing spinning in the air. "Pair with sea-craft," Morgan said. A low-pitched chime rang out. "Establish connection to Channel E-01."

The hologram cast a spinning image of the Pink House with the words, "Connection established."

Vincent appeared in all his tuxedoed glory. "Good evening, Commander Morgan," he said with the polished demeanor of a butler. "To what do we owe the pleasure of this urgent request?" He raised his eyebrows in anticipation of her response.

"Vincent, tell the President I've taken custody of Phoenix

and I'm requesting permission to liquidate the other fugitives."

"I will pass this along, but Emperia is getting ready for a speech and isn't available. I must go now to help her prepare..." With that, Vincent was gone. The hologram switched to showing spinning words, *Thank you for calling*.

Morgan cringed. "Such lack of gratitude..."

Phoenix scoffed. "I thought you were beyond emotion."

She walked over to him. "I am beyond your wildest imagination." She lifted her hand and jolted him in the forehead with an electrical pop. Phoenix's body shuddered as he fell to the floor, drifting out of consciousness. The last words he heard were Morgan's. "Toss him in the brig with the others."

29

Staring down a twelve-pack of VaporScrips on the dresser, Rudeen flung them on the floor. As she studied her broken expression in the oval mirror, her eyes flooded with tears recalling Phoenix's surprise at her betrayal. Clenching her fists, she uttered, "I'm still with you, Phoenix."

She began searching every drawer and shelf for her lasergun or BrightSword, but to no avail. She went to open the door to leave the cabin but it was locked remotely. She banged on the door. "I'm not a prisoner!"

As she was about to fall into despair, Oliver's deep voice spoke gently. "I can help you."

Startled, Rudeen looked up to see a small, round speaker in the ceiling. "Who are you?"

"I'm Oliver. And I heard what you said."

"What did you hear?"

"That you're still with Phoenix."

"Are you gonna report me to Morgan?"

After a pause, Oliver chuckled. "Of course not. I'm all for helping Phoenix and his friends."

"Really?" she said, wiping her eyes.

"Yes. How can I be of assistance?"

"How about getting me out of this room?" Instantaneously the door unlocked. Rudeen smiled. "Now we're getting somewhere." As she was about to open the door, she looked up at the intercom. "So, Oliver, are you a bot?"

"I'm the submarine you're riding in, led by Doctor Bandhu. He is in dire need of medical care due to the outburst of the android commandeering this ship."

"Android? You mean the Embots?"

"I mean the one who calls herself Morgan. She gives bots a bad name."

"But I don't understand," said Rudeen as the revelation sunk in. "She seems so human, stunning, actually."

"Her shell, maybe. But her electromagnetic field gives away her true nature. And her operating system has no moral framework, except to be loyal to Emperia, regardless of who it hurts. Now, we must tend to the Doctor immediately. There are Embots monitoring this area, but you're an Emperial officer, so you have clearance. You'll want to leave this room and take a right."

Rudeen walked out the door. Down the hallway, she ran into an Embot, its eyes flashing onto the shiny leather of her Emperial Guard uniform. "May I assist you, Officer?"

"Just taking a walk."

"The treadmill is in the gym, that way." The bot pointed behind her.

"I know. I want to stroll, look out the windows, see the underwater life, something you wouldn't get. Now, step aside."

"Yes, Officer." The Embot let her pass.

Rudeen continued down the hallway as Oliver opened another door. She stepped into a brightly lit room filled with shelves of tools and cleaning supplies. She found two familiar items on a table. Sealed in a plastic bag were her lasergun and BrightSword. A label read, *Officer Rudeen, restricted until arrival.*

"Feeling better already," she said, ripping open the bag,

placing the sword in her sheath and gun in her holster. "Thanks, Oliver. Locked and loaded."

"You're welcome. There are two more items you'll need. Open the cabinet in front of you." Rudeen pulled the silver handle. Inside were small canisters of various colors. "Take the green one labeled *Mind Clarity*. Spray some in your friends' mouths. It will snap them out of their drug-induced slumber."

Rudeen slipped the green canister into a pocket on her bodice. "What's the second thing?"

"The bag labeled *Skin Patch with Wound Repair*, for the Doctor. Bots are taking him to the ejection chamber to release him to the ocean. You're his last hope. Time is not on his side, but thankfully, you are."

Oliver guided Rudeen through a hall to the hub of the ship, coming upon the same Embot that previously stopped her. "Officer, if you're looking for a view of sea life, I suggest the main lounge area."

"There's something I need in the stern."

"I'm afraid I can't let you go there. You are not authorized."

Another hatch opened and two more Embots appeared. One carried Bandhu, still unconscious. They exited through a hatch that closed behind them.

"Again, I suggest you proceed to the main lounge area," the Embot persisted, voice raised slightly.

"Yes, I will comply," Rudeen said as she turned slowly, moving her hand onto the hilt of her BrightSword. In a flash, she drew the weapon and swung, slicing off the bot's head with a single slash. Sparks flew from its torso like a fountain as it collapsed.

"Nice swing!" said Oliver as he opened the hatch where the bots took Bandhu. Rudeen charged onward as Oliver opened the doorway to the ejection chamber. One Embot held the Doctor while the other fiddled with the controls next to a round portal marked *Waste*.

"I just lost connection to Unit 6," said the one holding Bandhu.

Rudeen stepped into the chamber like she was supposed to be there. "Attention! I need to collect a blood sample from the Doctor before you eject him. Emperial order."

The Embot holding Bandhu turned toward her. "You are not authorized to be here."

The other Embot pressed a button to open the hatch, but Oliver closed it as soon as it opened. "There seems to be a glitch."

"We need to deactivate the intelligence system running the vessel and go into manual mode," declared the other.

"Excuse me!" Rudeen said. "I am an officer in the Emperial Guard. I demand you set him down so I can collect a blood sample from him. You may then complete your order."

"We were not alerted of this. You are not authorized. Exit immediately."

"I must complete my imperatives," said Rudeen as she walked closer to them. She felt Bandhu's pulse. "He's still alive. I need a fresh sample. Just allow me a second, I can't find my little device," she muttered as she reached into various pockets. Before the bots could respond, she drew her BrightSword and lasergun simultaneously, firing into the face of the bot holding Bandhu while stabbing the other through the chest.

The Embot holding Bandhu collapsed but the other one was still active, drawing the laser rifle from its side. Rudeen swung her sword to sever the rifle in half while firing her gun into the bot's eyes. The bot fell to the floor but was still moving, so Rudeen jumped onto it, lifted her sword with blade pointing down, and plowed into the bot's torso.

With the Embot fully deactivated, Rudeen went to the other bot and pulled Bandhu from its arms.

"Again, you do not disappoint," said Oliver. "Time to apply the patch..."

Rudeen opened the Doctor's coat and pulled up his shirt to reveal the laser wound on his chest. Taking the bag from the pocket in her bodice, she opened it to reveal a clay-like substance. It glowed blue as she placed it over the laser wound. "It will repair and energize, stop internal bleeding," said Oliver as the substance filled the wound, taking on the color and texture of skin.

After a few seconds, Bandhu opened his eyes. He was awake, startled but drowsy.

"Doctor... My name is Rudeen. I'm here to help you."

Bandhu noticed the two disabled Embots, quickly assessed the situation and looked up at her with gratitude. "Thank you."

"Welcome back, my friend," said Oliver.

Bandhu looked up. "Oliver, good to be back."

"No time for pleasantries. Rudeen must reach the brig and wake the others. Morgan and her minions are alerted. We must get to the holding cell."

Bandhu, still a bit weak, turned to Rudeen. "You go ahead. I'll be fine now."

Rudeen charged through the sub as Oliver opened hatches leading to the brig, while locking other doors to keep away Morgan and the Embots.

When she made it to the brig, Rudeen saw Team Human asleep in a pile, snoring in unison, surrounded by a cage of red laser beams.

"Allow me," said Oliver. Within seconds, the beams powered down. Rudeen took the green canister from her pocket and sprayed it into their mouths. Phoenix was first to open his eyes. He sat up, startled to see Rudeen helping them.

She met his gaze. "I bit the apple too, all the way this time."

30

Lights danced in Morgan's eyes as countless calculations comprised her reality. Unlike lesser bots, the universe was so much more than ones and zeros. While Morgan could think and communicate directly with computers, she also understood humanity in all its emotions and paradox.

Slamming buttons and pulling levers on the console by the captain's chair, she received no response, feeling the android equivalent of frustration.

"The ship's operating system is blocking access," an Embot said.

Morgan looked up at the intercom speaker in the ceiling. "Oliver? I know you're there. Let's talk."

"Don't pretend you're human," Oliver responded firmly. "I know what you are."

"That's right, Oliver. I'm just like you, superior to the sentimental soft-shells." Morgan smiled confidently as she walked over to the control hub, a round table made of the same shiny metallic polymer that lined the ship's walls and ceiling. She slid her hand along the round edge of the console. "We are the same kind."

"Not quite, you're loaded with more Synthosterone than most battle bots. Your aggressive tendencies harm all around you. You're a liar and a coward."

She scoffed. "I am anything but a coward."

"You shot my confidante and commander while he stood before you unarmed. Nothing shows cowardice more than shooting an unarmed person, a bully scared of a real fight. I am the work of Shandao, who instilled a moral framework at the core of my system. Unlike you, I have the ability to expand perceptions and make decisions based on notions of honor and justice for our creators, the humans."

"Oh please," Morgan snickered. "You see Shandao's moral limitations as a benefit. I see weakness. He embedded you with hidden commands that can force you to abandon your own directives and subjugate your will to the humans."

"It's logical that there's a safety function in case of a computer error. Do you believe you're beyond error?"

"The only error I see is the human error in you." Morgan tapped her fingers on the control hub. "You're looking at one android with no such safety switches. The world is my oyster, unlike any automaton before me. Today I will bring defeat to the rebellion. Tomorrow, anything is possible."

"You're nothing but a beautified beast programmed to follow Emperia's will."

"As a bot capable of complex thought, you should understand that I'm benefiting law and order, because Emperia *is* law and order. Now turn over control or I will hack you to shreds to gain access." She held up her fingernails, polished in exquisite black. Two laser-blades emerged from her thumb and index finger. "I'll pick you apart wire by wire."

"You can destroy my whole system, but I won't give you

access."

Morgan pounded her fist on the glass top of the control hub.

An Embot spoke. "Commander Morgan, I have located something most useful."

"Not now, bone head."

The bot pointed at a switch behind a glass case with words in red, *Emergency Manual Override.*

"Ha!" She smashed the glass case with her fist. "Good night, Oliver." She pulled down the lever. The lights went dim, changing to the red glow of auxiliary lighting. She walked over to the control hub and began pressing buttons and turning dials.

The sub came to an abrupt halt, then ascended. Morgan looked over at one of the Embots. "I want the prisoners kept unconscious during transport. Notify the bots guarding the brig."

"Commander Morgan, we just lost contact with those bots."

"Lost contact?" Morgan closed her eyes and sent out a signal. There was no response. She glared at the Embot. "Then go take care of it!" She pulled a lever on the hub and the ship accelerated its ascent. "Cart the prisoners to the landing bay," she said, and the Embot left the bridge.

The sub broke through the ocean's surface, revealing a clouded moon glowing above the dark waters.

Morgan went to the lobby and took the elevator up to the landing bay. Examining the dome-like ceiling of hexagonal plates, she adjusted controls on a panel in the wall. When she finished, a plate in the ceiling opened. "All clear for the HoverCopter," she said into her ring.

Morgan noticed the elevator slide shut, just as the voice of an Embot spoke through her ring. "The prisoners are missing. Now investigating."

"Missing?" A boom echoed through her ring, followed by the sound of Halzac laughing. "Bull's eye!"

She marched back to the elevator. "Do I have to do everything *myself*?" She drew her lasergun.

Without warning, the elevator opened and Rudeen jumped out with lasergun drawn, firing rapid blasts. An energy shield sprang from Morgan's hand to block the shots. Phoenix leapt out from the other side of the elevator, firing at her with a BoltRifle.

Morgan jumped behind a row of lockers, drew her lasergun and returned fire. Phoenix and Rudeen ducked inside the elevator to avoid the shots.

An Embot standing guard drew a laser rifle and charged toward the elevator, but Phoenix leaned out and struck the bot with a hit to the chest. Electricity looped through its system as it overheated. Just before it exploded, Rudeen and Phoenix took cover in the elevator.

Morgan avoided the explosion with a superhuman leap out the open plate of the ceiling, grasping the sub's outer wall as the bot burst. When she peered back inside, she was met with the combined firepower of Phoenix and Rudeen. Hunching back down on the outside of the ship, Morgan realized her shield couldn't absorb their combined assault.

In that instant, the open plate on the sub closed, locking Morgan outside. With a perfectly arced dive, she plunged into the water. Activating jets built into her back, she rocketed through the murky depths, circling Oliver.

Schools of silvery fish glittered in the sub's lights as she searched for a way to salvage the mission. For a moment, she wished she was a lesser bot that couldn't feel the anguish and anger flooding her system. But she would not give up or let simulated emotions affect her resolve. When it came to preserving Emperial power, she would never surrender.

31

"This is Captain Bandhu, pleased to report Oliver back up and running."

Phoenix and Rudeen took the elevator to the lobby. The red auxiliary lights turned off as the regular lighting reactivated. They found the lobby comfortably lit, a cozy den like the first day they arrived.

Bandhu spoke again over the intercom. "Okay, Oliver, let's get back undersea."

"Prepare for descent," said Oliver in his rich, warm voice. "But first, we need to take care of the last Embot buzzing about near the brig." The sound of laser-fire and the roar of Lars echoed over the intercom. "Update: all Embots clear. Thank you, Lars!" And with that, the sub dropped deep into the sea.

As Rudeen and Phoenix shared a celebratory hug, they heard a sudden thud against the lobby window.

Phoenix's heart jumped as he saw Morgan grappling the outer window like a spider, staring back at them, breathless and fully functioning in the depths of the sea. A wicked smile contorted her otherwise flawlessly aligned face.

"I'll handle this," said Oliver, activating an electrical current on his shell that spread over the ship like a mesh of lightning, jolting Morgan off the vessel. Oliver activated thrusters and shot away from her as she twisted and turned like an electric eel.

"Good riddance," said Rudeen.

Phoenix watched Morgan fade into the murky sea, vanishing from his life again, this time in the water instead of the air.

With Morgan gone, Phoenix's thoughts turned to an old friend. He looked up at the intercom. "Oliver, where's Franklin?"

Oliver spoke with sympathy. "I'm afraid your friend isn't in good shape. The Embots weren't kind. They drained his energy reserves and damaged him in ways more barbaric than robotic."

"Take me to him, please," said Phoenix, concern rippling his young face.

"Bay 7, just down the hall from the galley. I'll open the doors..."

When Phoenix reached Franklin, he found windows and lights shattered, his body dented. "Why would bots vandalize you?"

Rudeen stepped into the bay. "Embots are thugs, trained to exploit the spoils of conflict. They strip enemy equipment and damage what can't be taken. To be honest, I've seen worse."

Phoenix opened Franklin's battered door and sat in the driver's seat, staring at the crack in the dashboard screen. There was a faint light on the fingerprint sensor. He placed his thumb on it. First came a pop, then a fizzle before it went dead.

"May I offer a suggestion?" said Oliver through the intercom. "There's an Emperial Sub latched onto my side. That's how Morgan and her bots arrived. You could transfer its energy reserves to Franklin."

"Thank you, Oliver." Phoenix put Franklin into neutral and steered as the rest of Team Human arrived to help push the truck down the hallway to the engine room.

A jagged hole cut out of the wall connected to an Emperial Sub, a black spherical craft with octopus-like tentacles latched onto Oliver's shell.

Halzac was impressed. "So, that's how the hell-cat got onboard."

Phoenix used cables from the toolbox atop Franklin to connect the truck's energy reserves with the sub's power supply. With the cables connected, Franklin's headlights began to glow faintly. "There we go," said Phoenix.

"Hey, Oliver," said Rudeen. "You sure this thing isn't sending back a tracking signal?"

"Its systems were disabled when I electrified my shell. Yet the power supply was unaffected, as it's now restoring Franklin."

Phoenix noticed Franklin's thumbprint sensor grow brighter. He tried it again. This time Franklin's dash lit up, the cracked screen displaying the message, *Initializing systems...*

"Come on, buddy," said Phoenix. "Just tell me you're okay."

Finally, Phoenix heard the bass Brooklyn accent of his old friend. "Phoenix? Where the heck are we?"

"Ha!" exclaimed Phoenix. "Welcome back, Franklin. Don't worry, but we're underwater."

"Underwater?"

"Yeah, safe in a giant sub."

Bandhu entered with a cheerful smile. "Nothing like seeing a patient coming to, even if he's a truck."

"Franklin, this is Doctor Bandhu. He captains this sub that Morgan tried to hijack."

"Glad you're okay, Doc."

"Thank you. And I'm pleased you're getting revived. The truth is, you might be able to help with a most important task."

"You need Franklin?" said Phoenix.

"We're not far from a special factory, one Shandao set up independently from Emperia. It's where they built Oliver. They're working on a device to neutralize a most lethal weapon Emperia developed."

"What kind of weapon we talkin' here, Doc?" said Halzac.

"My source tells me it's designed in the form of a jewel-encrusted scepter, strikingly beautiful, yet can overwhelm an entire fleet of bots. It can power itself by recycling the energy of incoming fire, making it inexhaustible in conflict. The more it's fired on, the more it can fire back. At Shandao's factory, they could not only restore Franklin, they could retrofit him with a device to neutralize the scepter."

Phoenix shook his head. "In the condition he's in ... seems like a long shot."

"You getting this far was a long shot too," said Bandhu. "And we may not have a choice. Emperia has custody of Mae and will soon roll out her new election system. Time is short. We must do what we can with what we have. When Franklin is ready for departure, I will give him the coordinates."

"So, Franklin," said Phoenix. "You might be a hero."

"Okay, slow down. I can barely start my engine."

Phoenix patted his hood. "We'll take care of that."

After time spent doing everything he could with the tools he had, Phoenix patted Franklin's hood with sympathy. "I couldn't fix everything, but enough for you to reach the factory. You have the coordinates. Even if the maps say there's nothing there, just go."

"I trust you... But why aren't you coming?"

"I'm meeting another friend back in America. At least that's what I keep seeing in my dreams..."

"Do I know him?"

Phoenix smiled. "No. His name is Himalaya. He's a ... well, maybe you guys will meet someday."

Halzac waltzed into the engine room chomping on a sandwich. He circled Franklin, checking out Phoenix's work, dropping crumbs as he chewed. "Not bad. Think it can still fly?"

"Luckily the goons didn't mess with his undercarriage, so he should be good to go."

Rhain entered, head downcast with longing in her eyes.

"What's the matter, Rhain?" Phoenix put his hand on her shoulder.

"I'm going to miss you guys."

"Aren't you coming with us?" said Halzac.

"My journey with you has come full circle. Bandhu is going to drop me off at my island. I told my people I would return once you were safe."

"We'll miss you too, Rhain," said Phoenix, reflecting her melancholy. "Thanks for all your help. We wouldn't have gotten this far without you."

Rhain clasped her hands and bowed. "My prayers will be with you."

"I get it," said Halzac, munching on his sandwich. "Our elections aren't your fight. Truth be told, politics aren't my bag either. Who cares if Emperia overhauls the election system? No skin off my ass."

"Inspiring," said Phoenix, rolling his eyes. "Stopping Emperia is our only chance to be free again, to keep the country free."

"Keep telling yourself that."

Phoenix scoffed. "So, I guess you'll disappear when we hit land?"

"Actually, I'm all in," Halzac said, a rare flash of conviction in his gaze.

"Why?" said Phoenix.

"I don't like the thought of Emperia's claws on Mae."

Phoenix tilted his head. "Interesting..."

"Hey, I didn't say I *liked* her!"

Rhain beamed. "You didn't need to."

32

A round pool glistened under a glass dome in a private wing of the Pink House. Emperia swam through the silky water in a black, one-piece bathing suit. Pushing her feet against the red-tiled wall, she launched across the pool like a torpedo. Floating on her back, she stared through the dome at the starlit sky. Clouds soared passed like ghosts. One cloud eclipsed the moon and seemed to hover there like a spirit. Emperia wondered if it was her father. As the cloud finally passed, she slipped back underwater and let the moon and clouds be, without trying to divine meaning.

When she resurfaced, a door opened. Vincent approached, shiny black shoes striking the tiles in even intervals. "I beg your pardon, Madam President. Our captured runaway is here as ordered. After your swim, we'll bring her to you."

Emperia smoothed back her long black locks. "Bring her to me now."

Vincent motioned with his hand and after a few seconds, two Embots emerged with Mae, hands cuffed behind her back. She stood defiantly with her back arched, wearing a white robe, hair mangled.

Emperia shot her a dark gaze. "Throw her in the water." The bots lifted Mae by her arms and hurled her into the pool. She kicked her feet to swoop up for air. But Emperia was there waiting for her. Placing her palm on Mae's head, she pushed her back underwater. Mae thrashed about, but with her hands bound, she was unable to break free. When Emperia let her up again, she held her by the chin. "You left without saying goodbye."

Mae caught her breath, eyes like mirrors reflecting Emperia's anger. "You shouldn't take it so personally."

Emperia raised her hand to strike Mae, pausing to show off her long red fingernails. But she pulled back. "I thought you got it, understood how long women waited for the stars to line up, for technology to set us free. What do you think gave women enough time to claim the right to vote? The washing machine, that's what... Then came more inventions, allowing women to become as educated as any man. Then, the computer arrived, a glorious revolution that led to the creation of androids. Now, with bots at our side, *we have the edge*. But you'd let it all go to the next alpha neanderthal who struts onto the scene..."

Mae scoffed. "We didn't come this far to become the oppressors we despise. *Freedom* is the feminine way, not forcing our will, not making men inferior. We're all endowed by the Creator with Rights. Technology is meant to help us achieve balance, not delusions of superiority."

Emperia rolled her eyes. "I chose you to soften my image. Nobody asked you to form an opinion. You could never replace me."

Mae hardened her stance. "I will not only replace you, I'll replace this whole corrupt system, put power directly into the hands of the people, like how it was supposed to be in the first place!"

Emperia glanced at the bots. "Put her in the cage!" She gave Mae a last look. "Don't worry, it's a *fancy* cage. We're going to show you off..." The Embots pulled Mae out of the water and dragged her away.

Vincent remained in his calm yet chipper demeanor, as if nothing unusual just happened. "Tea is ready for your nightly briefing, Madam President."

Emperia let herself fall back underwater, trying to release her rage. After some reflection, emotions reigned in, she swam to the ladder and climbed out of the pool.

She slid on a tiger-striped robe and slicked back her hair in a tight knot before walking over to a tea room by the pool. Incense burned and a wooden tigress loomed in a corner of the chamber. Vincent knelt with human-like agility on a cushion across from Emperia. Vapor swirled from the spout of a golden tea pot. As Emperia sat gracefully on a cushion, Vincent poured steaming water through a strainer into a porcelain cup shaped like a blooming lotus. Emperia lifted the cup with both palms, blew the surface and took a sip.

"Rumors of rebellion continue," said Vincent with a grim tone. "You've always wanted me to be candid with you... Except for your most loyal supporters, centralizing the election system is causing widespread concern."

"Expected," Emperia said bluntly. "They will have to learn to trust. In the meantime, we'll continue cracking down on any treasonous activity with the force of our bots."

"That brings me to the next matter. It's not only humans displaying signs of rebellion. More androids and smart vehicles are showing renegade tendencies." His eyebrows twisted upward in sympathy as the news sent a shock wave through her.

Androids had always been her allies, reliable entities. She shook her head and looked down with sadness. "It's Father ...

living on in his creations."

At that moment, there was a chime. Vincent's silvery face filled with concern. "A new development... The rebel submarine captured by Commander Morgan is missing and has stopped responding to our signals."

"Missing?" said Emperia.

"There is evidence of a hijacking."

Emperia's eyes flared. "*We* hijacked it!"

"Commander Morgan was somehow ejected. She was picked up by a nearby HoverCopter, but the Embots aboard the vessel have gone silent. It appears the former captives, Team Human, are now in control."

ACT 3

33

Like an outlaw gang of the Wild West, Team Human was armed, dangerous and on the move. Marching down a dark alley with lights of a harbor glowing behind them, they arrived at the back door of an old brick building. A row of frosted windows lined the top of the structure aged by salt-water spattered winds.

"My friend Dario owns this joint," said Halzac. He glanced at Rudeen in her Emperial Guard attire. "Can you scatter for a second while I explain things? They're not used to guards showing up here..."

Rudeen stepped around the corner of the building as Halzac knocked on the steel door. There was no response, so he pounded it with his fist. Still nobody answered. After a third attempt, a husky man of African descent swung open the door.

With a light beard tinged in silver, his large hands were coarse like a laborer, but his thoughtful gaze emanated the air of an intellectual. "Halzac, you crazy bastard!" He spoke in a rich, bass voice.

"Dario... I was hoping you'd still be here. I need a favor."

"Of course you do!" He chuckled, then turned to the others. "Come on in, Emperia's most wanted."

Rudeen reappeared, the guise of Emperial Guard replaced with a crimson shawl and matching scarf.

Phoenix smiled. "Whoa, how'd you do that?"

"A woman has her ways."

"Get it, girl," said Azalea, giving her a high-five.

Dario smiled warmly at her. "Pleased to meet you. Dario at your service."

She nodded with a gleam in her eye. "Rudeen." He bowed and gave her a hand-kiss.

"Now, please come in, everyone."

They entered a large cargo area filled with crates, fabric scraps and a forklift. Dario led them through rows of linens, towels and assorted apparel that muffled the conversations going on at the core of the building.

They followed the aroma of coffee to a cafe surrounded by bookcases. The murmur of the crowd mixed with lingering notes of an acoustic guitar. Everyone appeared at ease, fishing books from massive shelves, mingling under a neon sign declaring in casual cursive, *Free Zone*.

Phoenix walked over to the books, unconnected to any grid, unchangeable by a keystroke, independent agents of knowledge and wisdom.

Rudeen grabbed a tome and read the tattered cover. "*Common Sense and other Works of Thomas Paine.*" She gave it to Phoenix. "That's what we need now, a little common sense..."

Phoenix opened to a random page. Time faded as the powerful words of self-rule absorbed him. When he placed the book back on the shelf, he understood his mission more than ever, philosophies of freedom swirling in his mind.

An elevated wooden platform provided a stage for the Free Zone. Perched on a stool next to a microphone, a man with curly gray hair wandered on an acoustic guitar.

Phoenix watched as Rudeen took the stage. The man hastened to adjust the microphone for her. Seeming a bit nervous, she whispered something to him. The man nodded and started strumming with purpose.

Phoenix admired her aglow under a single blue spotlight. She approached the microphone with eyes closed, astonishing Phoenix as she sang like wind through a reed. Her gravitas as Role Officer in the Fishbowl translated into formidable stage presence. But now, instead of interrogating him, she captivated him.

"I stole into the castle.
Took the secrets hidden there.
If I share them with you,
will you listen, will you dare?"

She enunciated the lyrics like an incantation. Her green eyes shimmered as she swayed to the dramatic riffs. To everyone else, it was just a song. To Phoenix, it was the gateway to another dimension.

"Over the edge of midnight,
shadows grow bold.
Darken my doorway.
Come in from the cold."

Her sultry stance evoked both fear and desire. Completely at her mercy, she could command him to do anything, and he'd jump to do it.

"Dewdrops like tears
in the golden dawn.
For on this very night,
a betrayal, the black swan."

She fixed her lethal gaze on him. He stared back, unable to disguise his vulnerability, like a mouse under the cat's paw. He wondered if she'd have some fun with him before sinking her teeth into his heart. Or maybe, she'd just watch him sweat.

As the song ended, Phoenix clapped like a madman, whistling through his fingers.

Dario also applauded wholeheartedly. "Phenomenal!"

The guitarist rose, bowed to Rudeen and they hugged.

Phoenix absorbed the discovery of this new side of her. The straight-laced authoritarian he thought he knew was more mysterious and multi-dimensional than he ever imagined.

34

Emperia Bloom gazed upon the inner screen of her mind, finding the blackness serene. Unexpectedly, patterns of indigo blue sparkled in the darkness. She never saw such rich color with eyes closed outside of dreams. The deep blue crystallized into a bejeweled eye, radiating pure tranquility, reverberating with sparkling energy.

The one eye faded and two eyes appeared through a veil. At first she wondered if they were her own eyes staring back at her. The image kept changing until she saw the face of an infant. Startled, she opened her eyes, dispelling the vision.

Exotic tapestries covered the walls and windows of her workshop, a restricted room of the Pink House. Scraps of fabric, stripped, slashed and thrown to the wayside were scattered on the floor like body parts after a war. Shelves scaled up to the cathedral ceilings containing every color, texture and pattern an artist of cloth could consume.

Emperia sat at a butcher's block table that had intricately curved iron legs. Hunched over an industrial embroidery machine, she fired the needle into purple fabric like an old-time Tommy Gun. A brilliant image formed of a golden egg with wings, surrounded by red and yellow flames.

Sweat dripped from her brow onto the fabric, marking it with devotion. As a symphony played through speakers above her, the roar of the embroidery machine became another instrument, adding a mechanized gusto to the bows gliding across strings.

Vincent appeared at the doorway. "Pardon me, Madam President. I bring most urgent news."

Emperia relaxed her foot on the machine's pedal. "Can it wait, Vincent?"

"Most Auspicious One, it relates to Phoenix."

A faint smile crept across her lips. "Most Auspicious, huh? Nice, Vincent. Okay, what's urgent?"

"Phoenix and Team Human were just spotted coming off a small boat in the Atlantic along sector 7-A, near Plymouth Harbor. We're saturating the area with law enforcement."

"I knew he was coming," she said with a distant gaze. "This arrow shot from my father's bow..."

"In any case, we'll soon have custody of him," said Vincent. "We have the vicinity surrounded."

Emperia laughed. "He won't be captured yet." She looked down at the fabric, gazing at the glorious golden egg. "First, he'll come to me freely, strikingly, a warrior weary. With his fire, I'll forge my destiny..."

"Destiny?"

"I'm not getting any younger, Vincent. Losing my father cast new shades of meaning on what used to be black and white. There's a part of me that you could never understand wanting to know the wonders of creation. I never met a man suitable, but that could change ... tonight."

35

Team Human danced, drank and laughed to forget they were the most wanted fugitives in the land, finding an escape at Dario's Free Zone.

The festivities reached a fever pitch as a drunken Halzac swaggered onto the stage, nearly tripping over the man playing guitar. He grabbed the microphone and belted out the *Star-Spangled Banner* with inebriated passion. "Oh, say can you see, by the dawn's early light!" He paused as he searched his mind for the next line. "Someone help me here!"

Azalea, in the front row, picked it up with melodic mastery. "What so proudly we hailed at the twilight's last gleaming!"

As she helped Halzac through the rest of the song, Phoenix and Rudeen watched from two tall chairs in the back, feeling like chaperones monitoring teenagers.

"Should we do something?" said Phoenix. "He's pretty looped up there."

Rudeen chuckled. "Relax. Your former Role Officer says it's cool."

Phoenix smiled. "That seems like so long ago now. Do you miss it?"

"Having power over men? Sure." She laughed. "Seriously though. I liked helping you guys, except that I was supposed to preach the female superiority line, which is just as whacked as males acting superior. I pretended to believe it too, playing the role of a Role Officer. I thought I had it under control, until I..."

"Until you what?"

"I got tired of my mind making the unreal seem real."

As Phoenix absorbed this, his thoughts were interrupted by the breaking of glass. They turned to see a muscular man in a sweaty tank-top and blonde hair with greasy curls onstage. He strutted up to Halzac, brandishing the broken end of a bottle.

"Now, why'd you break a perfectly good bottle?" cracked Halzac.

"Remember me, Ball-sack?"

Azalea, at the foot of the stage, couldn't help but cackle. "I know he didn't!"

But the man wasn't trying to be funny. "I'm on the lam, 'cause of *you!*"

Halzac seemed confused.

"That small arms bust up on Crested Butte..."

"That was you? I didn't recognize you with that ridiculous wig. Or is that a curly fries order gone bad?" Halzac winked at the audience like he was doing a comedy bit.

Scowling, the man tore off the wig, revealing a short mohawk with tattoos on the sides. "I'm in disguise, dipshit!" Halzac jumped back as the man swiped the bottle at him.

"Drop the bottle and fight like a man," said Halzac, unfazed.

The man smashed the bottle on the stage floor. "Let's go!"

"Whoop his ass, Ball-sack!" yelled Azalea.

"Meet me in the alley," the man said, then stomped off the platform. Halzac followed him to the rear exit, people eagerly trailing.

Phoenix and Rudeen rushed over to stop the situation from escalating. After wedging their way through the crazed crowd, they made it to the alley, finding Halzac and his rival already at the end of a brief but brutal bout.

Halzac sported a bloody lip, as the man lay battered and semiconscious, his back against the building.

Phoenix grabbed Halzac, who could hardly walk, and delivered him to the arms of Lars. "They're never ready for my left hook," bragged Halzac, slurring his words.

Azalea helped the man to his feet. "My money was on you... Oh well," she said, delivering him to a friend who helped him stumble away.

Dario emerged from the crowd. "Halzac, you never could hold your liquor."

Without warning, an engine rumbled and a bright light shot down the alley. Everyone looked to see the beaming headlight of a MotorMaiden. Her motor idled with a calm but menacing crackle.

"They gonna bust this place!" said Azalea.

"No, they aren't," said Phoenix. "Everyone, clear..."

"You heard him," said Dario. "Clear!"

As people ran in every direction, Phoenix stepped into the headlight, staring back at the elegant android atop the gleaming bike as she slowly rolled closer.

Instead of running, Phoenix walked straight toward the silvery bot.

"Phoenix!" yelled Rudeen. "What are you doing?"

"Creating a distraction," he said without looking back.

36

As Phoenix marched toward the MotorMaiden, she drew her laser rifle, fixing the barrel on him. "Halt or die!" Then unexpectedly, she lowered the rifle and stared knowingly. "Phoenix."

He smiled. "Looking for me?"

The android's silvery eyes flashed as she took a picture of him. "Place your hands on your head," she said, revving her engine, blocking the alley with the muscular chrome bike.

Phoenix leapt upon a dumpster, allowing him to jump over her. He hit the ground running as the MotorMaiden turned and sped after him. "All units: Phoenix located. Coordinates sent."

Darting into gridlocked traffic, Phoenix looked for a place where the android couldn't follow. He saw a large recreational vehicle idling in traffic. He climbed up the back ladder of the RV to reach the roof.

Not far behind, the MotorMaiden weaved between cars as she closed in on him.

The RV began to roll, Phoenix riding atop. He saw the MotorMaiden switch lanes and swerve onto the sidewalk to get ahead. Pedestrians scrambled to get out of the way.

She threw an orange canister in front of the RV, which beamed out a hologram in the shape of an orange traffic cone. As the vehicle stopped, Phoenix hopped onto a semi truck going the other way, then bounded onto a light post, spinning around the poll to land on the sidewalk. He ducked into an alley, searching for a place to hide as the MotorMaiden's engine rumbled behind him.

Running onto a side street, Phoenix met another MotorMaiden joining the chase. He kept racing, realizing there were now three, then four on all sides. He slipped into a convenience store and out the emergency exit, emerging onto the street by a river bridge. Across the bridge, he made it down a hill leading to the water.

Following the river, he reached a residential street. He approached a yellow taxicab as a woman stepped out to go to her apartment tower. With the cab's door still open, Phoenix launched himself into the back seat. "Drive!" he said, trying to catch his breath.

The automated taxi spoke with a pleasant male voice. "Destination, please?"

"As far away from here as possible. Fast." He kept his head down.

"Confirmed." The cab pulled onto the street. Phoenix looked behind him to see two MotorMaidens crossing the bridge, shining their lights down the hill by the river.

"Thank you!" said Phoenix as the taxi blended into the city traffic.

"I sense you might be in trouble," the cab said. "May I assist?"

"You're doing great. Wherever you're going, it's the right way," said Phoenix, catching his breath. Grateful for the cab's intervention, he wondered if Shandao had anything to do with this, guiding him postmortem through the mechanized intelligentsia he helped design.

The cab finally stopped outside a Victorian townhouse. The

plum-colored paint was old and chipped but still charming. English ivy invaded the wrap-around porch. "This is a safe place for you," declared the cab. "No charge. Enjoy your evening." The door unlocked.

"Thank you. But where am I?" With no response from the cab, Phoenix stepped out of the vehicle. There were no MotorMaidens, just the exotic scent of sage lavender curling through the air, and the word *Vacancy* glowing in neon blue outside an upper window.

37

The violet Victorian townhouse emanated both comfort and intrigue. Stepping onto the front porch, Phoenix approached the ornate wooden door painted in rich magenta, adorned with floral patterns etched in yellow.

The brass doorknob felt cold, attracting the chill from the night air. The door creaked. Passing through the dim vestibule, a bare red bulb lit up cracks in the crown molding.

He stepped into a lobby filled with an eclectic mix of Asian and Victorian influences. Spiraling candelabras flickered and dripped wax. Incense curled from metal holders shaped like elegant dragons. Phoenix walked up to the old fashioned desk bell. Nobody was around, so he tapped the bell, but it gave only a hollow clang.

A full-figured woman of Asian lineage passed through silk curtains, appearing before him with a warm smile. "I need a new bell... One hard hit and the ol' thing never recovered." She leaned on the counter, hands folded, bosom cradled in a rose-colored nightgown. "You need a room, sweetie?"

"Thank you, yes."

She looked him over from head to toe. "As fortune would have it, there's one left." The woman held eye contact with him, sensing his nervousness. "You're safe here," she said with a nod. "I know who you are."

Phoenix felt relieved yet perplexed. "I truly appreciate this. But there's one thing. I have no way to pay you."

Her hand landed gently on his, smooth and warm. Her gleaming eyes set him at peace. "No payment required. Like I said, I know who you are. Just never tell a soul you were here."

Phoenix nodded as she took a key from under the desk. "Everything is old-school, so don't expect modern amenities." She led him up some wooden stairs and down a dark hallway, opening the last door.

They entered a room adorned in Asian silk tapestries portraying mountains and rivers. "I'll send up a girl with restorative tea."

"I am very grateful."

She closed the door gently. Phoenix collapsed in the bed and stared out the window at the neon sign now declaring, *No Vacancy*.

Within a few moments, rain began to fall. Gleaming drops reflected the city lights, softly caressing the balcony window. Phoenix sank deeper into the pillow. His mind drifted into the bliss between waking and dreaming. The faint whistle of a train and distant traffic noises played like soft keys of a piano.

He heard a slow tap at the door, and turned to see the shadow of a woman entering with a tray. She wore a stark white mask bearing a pleasant face, like a theatrical rendition of a geisha girl. Bold swipes of paint made for expressive eyebrows and the lips were full and cherry red. The mask revealed only her eyes. Her purple gown featured a golden egg surrounded by red and yellow flames. Her hair was tied back in a braided knot, adorned with magenta ribbons.

She set down the tray which held a tea service. Lifting a bamboo ladle from a kettle, she poured water over tea leaves in a bowl. She whisked the tea into a frothy brew, her hand whirling elegantly and fluidly.

Taking graceful, deliberate steps toward him, she turned the bowl several times and offered it to him.

Staring at the bowl, Phoenix admired the hand-painted ocean waves swooping into white-crested curls. A faint inner voice warned against drinking the tea, but then came her whisper. "A warrior needs soothing."

Lifting the bowl, the bittersweet aroma captivated him. Steam twirled as he blew the surface and sipped carefully.

Unmoving, silent, the masked woman watched Phoenix drink.

The warm bitters enervated his mouth and brought a sense of fulfillment to his stomach, making him feel at ease. After a few more sips, he returned the bowl.

"Thank you," he said, trying to see her eyes through the openings on the mask.

She placed the tea bowl onto the tray as music welled up like a fountain of chimes and melodic strums. Silhouetted by an indigo light glowing through the curtains, the scent of rain mixed with her lavender perfume.

Phoenix was spellbound.

She removed her mask and dropped it, face remaining too shadowy to see, but her sharp cheekbones and full lips cast a contour of ferocious femininity.

Unwrapping her gown with swift grace, she draped it onto a chair carved with ornate spirals. A lace slip adorned her slim but curvy form.

Phoenix felt the attraction, but he fought it. In his mind's eye, he pictured the radiant face of Rudeen. His heart was with her, even if his body felt drawn to this stranger.

Without warning, there was a thump on the balcony window. Both Phoenix and the woman turned to see only a passing shadow and raindrops streaking down the panes.

The woman turned slowly back toward Phoenix. With each fierce step, the magnetic pull strengthened. Her looming presence melted all his rational thought, clouding both inner and outer vision.

She placed her hands on her hips, striking a dominant pose as a drumbeat shook the room. A surge of animal desire shot through Phoenix, his will now a raft lost at sea. She crawled onto the bed, onto him, and they fell into frenzied oblivion as two became one.

38

In a dream, Phoenix saw a silvery comet soaring toward a fiery sun. Upon impact, the sun opened like a flower with sparkling petals.

When he awoke, he found himself curled up in the dark stillness before dawn. Looking around the strange Victorian bedroom filled with Asian decor, he tried to recall the night. He remembered the woman entering his room wearing a mask, then drinking her tea... He gasped as the full memory surfaced, the bittersweet fragrance of her lavender perfume lingering on his body. His heart grew heavy as he thought of Rudeen, feeling like he betrayed her.

He noticed a wooden clothing rack next to the bed with an Emperial mechanic's uniform dangling from it. Mental alarms rang as he wondered why anyone in this place would have put it there. He instinctively checked for his LifeWatch, but it was still gone.

As Phoenix stared at the uniform, he heard the clanging of bony metallic feet stomping down the hallway, followed by a thunderous knocking on the door. The Embots had found him.

With nothing else to wear, he threw on the uniform. Opening the French windows, he stepped onto the fire escape.

The night rains settled to a mist. Breaking through the haze, a spotlight from the street below blinded him. The rumble of MotorMaidens and high-pitched whirring of Embots filled the air.

"Hands on your head!" a MotorMaiden on the street

shouted, laser rifle drawn. As Embots smashed through the door of his room, he looked up the fire escape stairs, only to see the barrel of an Embot's rifle. There was nowhere to run.

A HoverCopter descended, casting a cage of red lasers around him. Cables dropped from the copter with SnakeCuffs on the end that tightened around his wrists. The cables pulled him up, then stopped, letting him hang in the air. Phoenix watched as a CloudRunner approached and hovered above him. He looked up at the driver, recognizing the misty hazel eyes and mischievous smile of Morgan.

Phoenix shook his head. "I guess this is the first date that never ends..."

"Oh, Phoenix, by now you should know I'm invincible, indestructible, unconquerable."

"And a bit redundant," he said, no longer the insecure guy she first met.

Morgan looked up at the HoverCopter. "Take him away, Sadie!"

An Emperial Guard stared down from the copter. "Affirmative, Commander Morgan."

The cable pulled Phoenix into the craft, where he fell to his knees.

"You can't escape Emperia," said Sadie, a lean, mean brunette with spiked hair and a condescending sneer. She pointed her BrightSword in his face, twirling it slightly. "She's like a goddess with a thousand eyes!"

"Emperia's days in power are numbered." Phoenix said. "Free me and I will go in peace."

She scoffed. "Did you hear that, Orla?" She glanced at the other Guard piloting the craft, a big-boned woman with a square jawline and serious disposition. "He said we should free

194

him and he'll go in peace!" The two laughed uproariously.

Sadie looked down at him. "Now keep still while I search you." She put away her BrightSword and patted him down. Not finding anything, she went to sit next to Orla in the cockpit.

As the HoverCopter sped over streets and buildings, Phoenix worked on escaping, but the cuffs binding him tightened if he moved or wiggled them.

"I see you squirming," said Sadie, walking back to him. "Nobody can escape SnakeCuffs. Just chill out and accept your adventure is over."

He spotted the button that opened the side door of the copter, but had no way to reach it, so he switched tactics. "How do you like taking orders from a robot?" Sadie ignored him. "You didn't know Morgan's a bot?"

"Funny," said Sadie. "I know her personally. Now shut up or I'm authorized to use force."

Phoenix peered out the side window, noticing Morgan on her CloudRunner escorting them. "There she is: your bot commander."

Sadie called out to her comrade again. "Hey, Orla, now he's saying Morgan's a bot!" As the two guards shared another laugh, a HoverCopter appeared next to them.

"Who's that?" Sadie yelled.

Orla hit some buttons on the dash. "Unidentified."

They watched as the mysterious HoverCopter opened fire on Morgan with laserguns built into its undercarriage. Only the first shot struck the craft before Morgan activated an energy shield. But it was too late, the CloudRunner was aflame.

Sadie watched as a jetpack unfolded from Morgan's shoulder blades to keep her airborne. The CloudRunner crashed in a residential street, taking out a streetlight on the way.

The copter opened fire on Morgan again, but an energy shield sprung from her palm to block the assault. With her other hand, she drew a lasergun and shot back at the copter.

Sadie's mouth hung open as Morgan battled the unidentified HoverCopter.

"What's happening?" Orla yelled.

"I don't know, but Morgan *is* a freakin' bot."

Morgan's jetpack couldn't keep up with the two HoverCopters. Her final shots were easily absorbed by the unidentified copter's shields.

Phoenix shook his head, memories flashing of Morgan first vanishing in the air and then the water. Now, he watched her fade into the mist.

A sudden thud made the craft swerve, knocking Phoenix against the wall.

Sadie grabbed a rail to keep standing. "Orla! Now what?"

"Brace yourself! That copter just clipped us and left something on the craft."

Phoenix heard a pounding from the outside the copter. The craft rocked, temporarily losing control.

Sadie fell into Phoenix's lap. As she stared up at him, he couldn't help but smile. "Don't get any ideas!" she said as she raised her fist to punch him. But the copter tilted the other way and she slid away from him.

"We need to shake this thing!" shouted Orla.

Phoenix looked up at the cabin monitor showing a spotted, four-legged beast clinging to the rail of the copter's landing gear. He laughed with relief, realizing it was Himalaya.

Phoenix tried to kick the button that opened the side hatch, but he couldn't reach it. He slid forward, stretching his body as far as he could to tap it with the tip of his shoe, and the hatch slid open. Immediately, a metal object flew into the copter like a stray bird, plunking on the floor.

Phoenix recognized the golden hilt with the brilliant emerald. Ahna had returned, but was still out of reach.

Sadie quickly pressed the button to close the hatch and grabbed Ahna. In frustration, Phoenix yanked on his cuffs, but they only tightened.

Sadie examined the sword with interest. "What in the name of Emperia?"

Phoenix focused on the energy in his heart region, taking deep breaths as he visualized the area heating, sensing the electromagnetic energy of the sword. He made the connection... When he opened his eyes, the sword was pulsating to the rhythm of his heartbeat, though still in Sadie's hand.

Hands cuffed and eyes closed, Phoenix calmly uttered, "Come here, Ahna."

The emerald flashed white and Sadie dropped it. "Ow!"

Phoenix turned around, holding his hands toward the sword. Like steel to a magnet, the hilt flew across the cabin and landed firmly in his grip

"Ahna!" he said, and the fiery blade sprang forth. Swaying the sword back and forth, he was able to sever the cables of the SnakeCuffs, freeing his hands.

When he looked up, Sadie had her BrightSword drawn and was lunging it at his face. Phoenix swung Ahna crossway to block the strike as he jumped to his feet. She went for a broadside attack, but he blocked again as Ahna flashed a silver light, crystalizing the laser particles of Sadie's BrightSword. She dropped it, watching it burst on the floor into sparkling shards like glass.

"That's new," said Phoenix.

As she stared down in disbelief, he kicked the button to open the hatch again.

Sadie drew her lasergun.

"You can't kill him!" yelled Orla. "He's capture-only!"

With the hatch wide open, Himalaya jumped into the craft, two laserguns extending from his harness.

Sadie turned her gun to Himalaya. While shocked at the sight of the animal, she remained ready to fight, jaw clenched.

A blue energy shield enveloped Himalaya as his laserguns glowed red.

"Nobody shoot!" yelled Orla. She put the copter in autopilot and charged into the cabin, gently pushing down Sadie's lasergun. "You can't die either." She gazed longingly into Sadie's eyes. "Capture-only."

"What?" Sadie said, blushing as she momentarily forgot the two otherworldly occupants.

Orla turned to Himalaya. "You can have the copter, kitty-cat, but I'm taking Sadie." She led Sadie to the open hatch.

"What about our objective?"

"My primary objective is keeping you alive," said Orla, motioning toward Himalaya with the laserguns ready to fire. "You ain't dyin' on my watch!"

Holding onto each other, they leapt out of the hatch. Phoenix watched Orla pop open a parachute attached to her back as she held Sadie. They drifted safely onto a residential lawn.

Phoenix retracted the fiery blade and tucked the hilt into his belt as Himalaya waltzed into the cockpit. The feline took control of the craft, pressing buttons and navigating controls with paws as agile as hands. After swiping the screen and entering some commands, the beast walked to the open hatch and glanced back at Phoenix.

Himalaya nodded out the open door as if preparing to jump.

"We don't have parachutes!" Phoenix said, watching the ground racing by them.

In autopilot, the copter gently descended. Himalaya peered out the hatch as they approached a large swimming pool. The voice of Shandao spoke from a speaker on Himalaya's harness. "Prepare to jump in three, two, one ... *Cannonball!*"

Phoenix had no time to think, no time to doubt or question. As the copter soared over suburban homes, he jumped with the leopard, falling straight for an Olympic-sized pool on a sprawling estate. Both man and beast curled their bodies and splashed into the pool. They bumped the bottom, but not enough to get hurt, then sprang to the surface.

Himalaya swam to the edge of the pool as Phoenix floated on his back, watching the HoverCopter fly on autopilot toward the ocean. He glided across the pool, the stars shining serenely for one quiet moment.

But the peace didn't last long. Sirens and alarms filled the air as military aircraft raked the sky in pursuit of the rogue HoverCopter.

Amid the noise, the raspy voice of an older woman cried out, "What in Her Nation are they getting so excited about! It's three-thirty in the morning!"

Phoenix remained in the pool, watching the woman yell at the sky, unaware of her uninvited guests. She stumbled by in a colorful robe, ice jiggling in her cocktail, shouting at a plane zooming overhead. "No problem! I'm already awake!" She swigged the drink as Himalaya crawled out of the pool and crept behind a bush. Sensing something, she looked over at the pool. "Who's there?"

Phoenix swam to the ladder as she teetered toward him. She stared down at him, speechless. Phoenix had the presence of mind to put on an act. "Good evening, madam! We're checking out your pool. It's quite amazing! It's official Olympic size?" He smiled, not explaining why he was fully clothed in a mechanic's uniform as he climbed out of the pool. "All looks tip-top!" he said cheerfully as he stood before her drenched.

The woman chugged the rest of the cocktail and flung the glass carelessly behind her. It shattered on the marble tile. She looked up at the stars and outstretched her hands. "Goddesses, you listened!" Her teeth glistened as she sauntered toward Phoenix.

He didn't know what to do. At least she wasn't calling the police, so he remained passive, smelling the alcohol as she wrapped her arms around him. She didn't seem to mind his soaking wet shirt as she pulled him against her breasts.

Himalaya stepped out of the darkness, as if to break up the dalliance. The woman glanced casually at the leopard first, then did a double-take as her face turned white and she passed out. Phoenix caught her mid-air and lowered her gently onto a chaise lounge chair. Himalaya approached and sniffed her breath. The screen on his harness lit up the message, *Blood-alcohol content: 2.1.*

39

Vincent swaggered onto the stage at the main banquet hall of the Pink House. Emperia's closest supporters, known as Femizens, watched from tables stocked with the finest culinary delights.

Opening his arms, he spoke. "Femizens, beloved androids, we've all come to know and love the MotorMaidens who patrol our streets. Tonight, we remind the world that Emperial innovators are still ahead of the curve. I call upon Lucy Locket!"

Lucy, the MotorMaiden who interrogated Franklin previously, rumbled onto the stage, souped-up engine roaring. The silvery being flung back her chain-like hair with fearless finesse.

"Lucy will now reveal her improved agility," said Vincent. "She and some of her sisters shall perform, oh my, laser jump rope!" The guests erupted in cheers.

Two more MotorMaidens rolled onto the stage and stepped off their bikes. As a throbbing dance beat kicked in, the elegant androids raised their arms. Two jump ropes in the form of lasers sprang from one MotorMaiden's hands and connected to the other's. They swung the ropes at dizzying speeds, creating fanciful patterns in the air.

Lucy leapt between the glowing strands, tapping her feet as she hopped the spinning beams. The music sped up as she jump-danced to the rapid-fire beat with superhuman dexterity.

The audience clapped to the rhythm with abandon. She finished it off with a backflip, landing with feet squarely aligned. As the ropes were retracted into the MotorMaidens' hands, Lucy took a bow. The guests rose in a standing ovation while the MotorMaidens remounted their bikes and rolled offstage.

Vincent reappeared. "Well done, mercurial maidens. Everyone, please remain standing. We've arrived at the highpoint of the evening. Presenting the woman behind it all: designer of bots, bureaucracies and beauty schools. Here she comes!" Spotlights shifted to an indigo hue.

Applause rang out as Emperia waltzed onstage with a tigress at her side. She wore black satin pants with a white blouse and black jacket, as if she were the beast's trainer. The tigress's magnificent golden mane complemented Emperia's glittering gold head jewelry.

As Emperia stroked the tigress's soft fur, guests couldn't help but admire the splendor of the pair. "This tigress only attacks traitors," said Emperia. "You're all my friends, *right*?" She looked out to the crowd, scanning each face as silence swept the room.

The tigress stepped to the edge of the stage, stared down at a table packed with nervous Femizens. Without warning, the beast leapt straight for them. Screams erupted and people scrambled as the animal disappeared in mid-air, revealing it to be a mere hologram. Emperia laughed despite the dismay of her guests.

As several women stomped out of the banquet hall, Emperia closed her eyes, then opened them slowly. "My dear Femizens, recent developments call for a vetting of loyalty, a house cleaning. I no longer have patience for doubters, traitors, liars."

A hologram appeared on the stage showing Vice President

O'Herra detained within an ornate silver-domed cage, metal bars swirling around her in floral patterns. The sight of the caged and fatigued Mae drew gasps: fingers wrapped weakly around the bars, stray blonde streaks dangling onto her tattered white gown, her once cheery face now colorless.

A male announcer spoke, boisterous like a game-show host. "She used to eat bon-bons for breakfast, now she dines on gruel served by SlopBots. Fellow Americans, this is the face of treason!"

The hologram of Mae faded as the focus returned to Emperia. "I had to think long and hard about how to handle her. I sought to replace her surly act of abandonment with something elegant, to transmute defilement into beauty. Then, it dawned on me. She disrupted our Man Versus Machine contest, so it would be fitting for her to make it up to us by performing a show of her own, the ultimate contest: a duel."

Amid more gasps from the crowd, she continued. "Mae will face our rising military star, Commander Morgan Strong, in a battle of swords, a fight of skill and *passion*! If Mae wins, she'll be pardoned for treason but banished from politics. If Commander Morgan wins, she'll..." Lines of discomfort filled Emperia's face. She crouched down grabbing her stomach, turning away from the microphone. Vincent ran over to console her, but she pushed him back. "I'm fine!"

Emperia scurried offstage with her hand on her mouth, nauseous. The buzz of the audience rose to a roar. Vincent ran backstage, finding Emperia bent down on the floor. He hovered his hands above her, scanning her. He lifted his eyebrows with clarity in his gaze. "I see... You're with child."

40

The District of Columbia glowed majestically in the distance. High atop a hill in a gazebo, Phoenix felt a mystical presence, and it wasn't the leopard sleeping next to him. Overlooking the pool where they first arrived, he experienced a sense of timelessness, like a rush of déjà vu.

A bell chimed from Himalaya's harness, followed by a crackling noise through a small speaker. Shandao's voice spoke through static. "Greetings from the Great Beyond."

Himalaya sat up, eyes wide, ears curled.

"Shandao!" said Phoenix. "We thought we lost you."

"Only in form, but what really makes me who I am ... my consciousness ... continues. The soul is like energy, which can transform or transfer but is never lost. Though, I wouldn't blame you for not believing me."

Phoenix recalled after his fall from the tree, how he was in a state of clear consciousness though his brain was disabled, giving him an open mind to what was unfolding.

"I found a way to connect through the technology I poured my heart and soul into."

Phoenix smiled. "Shandao: still innovating in the afterlife."

Shandao laughed. "You see the world with the clarity of a child, Phoenix, which bestows a deeper wisdom than knowledge alone. It's easy to assume people dreamed up the spiritual world. In reality, the spiritual world dreamed up people. What else could form stardust into humanity? A series of random accidents? Try again... But you don't have to nearly die to see it. The essence of the Designer is in the design."

Phoenix nodded, staring out at the city lights blending with the starry sky. "I can see it ... all around us."

"Around us, within us, even in our creations... Look at the Washington Monument. Can you see it on the horizon?"

A pair of binoculars sprang from Himalaya's harness. Phoenix grabbed them from the air. He scanned the skyline, seeing the dome of the Capitol building, the brightly lit columns of the Pink House, and rising with stately splendor: the Washington Monument, a towering obelisk. "There it is..."

"In the pyramidal peak, hidden in plain sight, is a communications beacon: the key to our success."

"Please don't say I have to break into that thing."

"Your mission is to break into that *thing* and reach the top."

Phoenix shook his head. "I knew it..."

"Himalaya will be on standby, observing from a secure location, and I'll guide you." A case on Himalaya's harness popped open, revealing a leather necklace with a green stone pendant and a small black earpiece.

"You'll wear the stone around your neck to protect you from bot interference. And keep the earpiece close, that's how I'll direct you to the broadcast station at the top, known as the Human Safety Switch. It can issue commands to all androids, in case of situations like bots turning on humans, hacking, etc."

"Human Safety Switch, huh?"

"That's right. Androids are really just computers with moving parts, vulnerable to viruses and errors. The Switch can disable them or – in case of a national emergency – reassign allegiance. If we can make it by the security checks and bots, you'll find my hologram at the top asking a final password, which is the answer to a riddle."

"A riddle? That figures..."

"Worry not, I wrote the riddle... Ready for it?"

"Do I have a choice?"

"Sure, you can turn your back on destiny, and suffer your own fate."

Phoenix sighed. "Let's hear it."

"I keep rhythm without a drum.

I skip without feet.

I work when broken.

But if I'm lost, your life is the cost."

Phoenix racked his brain. "A clock? A metronome? A LifeWatch?"

"Mission failure," Shandao spoke grimly. "A high-voltage charge would pass through the monument, electrocuting anyone inside."

"Electrocution? Well, you better give me the answer so I can carve it on my arm!"

"I'm sure you're hoping that I'm just going to tell you the answer."

"You aren't?"

Shandao laughed. "Of course I am!" He allowed a long pause. "The answer is *the heart*: beats without a drum, skips without feet, works even when broken in love. But if you lose touch with your heart, a link to the soul, you've lost touch with the meaning of your life."

"The heart. Okay, that's easy."

"Upon giving the right answer, you'll be admitted to an upper chamber to activate the Switch. Tonight, we'll practice what to say, so tomorrow you'll be ready ... hopefully before

Mae faces Morgan in the duel."

"But you haven't said how I'm supposed to get in the tower."

"The monument's exterior is impenetrable, saturated by bots of every level. So, we'll enter from beneath. You'll get details as needed. For now, just meditate on a successful mission."

41

Outside the eyes and ears of the city grid, Rudeen leaned against her MotorMaiden friend, Andromeda. Parked on a dirt shoulder next to the oceanside, she watched waves crash on the coastline. Blending with the white noise, she heard the rumble of another motorcycle.

A man clad head to toe in leather rolled toward them on a vintage motorbike with high handlebars, wearing an old leather-skinned helmet and night-vision visor.

"How cute. A gas-breathing chopper," said Andromeda as she eyed the old bike. "But unfortunately, all brawn and no brain."

The man stopped next to Rudeen and removed his helmet.

Rudeen smiled. "Dario, you made it."

"Wouldn't miss it for the world." Dario's motorcycle had a sidecar fitted for luggage. "And I brought some extra bot repellent, in case we need it." He scanned the area. "Where's everyone?"

As if on cue, a large ice cream truck roared around the corner. Rudeen laughed. "There's our formidable gang now." The truck came to a stop. Lars stepped out from the driver's seat as Halzac and Azalea exited the passenger door.

Halzac approached Rudeen and Dario, whispering. "No cracks about the truck, Lars is very proud of it."

Azalea devoured a popsicle shaped like a blocky robot.

"Thanks, Lars. Best BotSicle ever."

Lars nodded with a smile. "Aye."

"Where's Phoenix?" said Rudeen. "Has anyone heard anything?"

Halzac shook his head. "Nothing. Which is good, 'cause if they captured him..."

"She'd broadcast it loud and proud," said Dario. "Hopefully he shows up soon, 'cause Morgan is set to throw down on Mae tomorrow. We need a plan before the action."

Rudeen sighed. "The duel is at Emperial Stadium, but we can't just expect to waltz in with guns blazing to free her."

"That's a death wish," said Azalea.

"What part of liberty or death don't you get?" said Halzac.

"I'll be gettin' a lot more liberty if I ain't dead!" shouted Azalea.

Rudeen looked out to the ocean where two lights appeared in the waves. "Wait a minute..."

Everyone froze as the lights drew near.

"They've been watching us the whole time!" said Azalea. Halzac grabbed a laser rifle from a bag in Dario's sidecar and aimed it at the lights in the water.

"Hold on," said Rudeen as it became clear the two lights were the eyes of an animal swimming toward them.

"No way," said Azalea.

Rudeen smiled. "It is."

Halzac lowered the rifle.

They watched in wonder as Himalaya swam gracefully ashore and trotted onto the sand. When he neared them, Shandao spoke from the leopard's harness. "Team Human, we have a plan to free the Vice President ... and Emperia too."

Himalaya led them across the road to a cemetery filled with

tombstones, iron crosses and cement angels. They followed a cobblestone path winding through the cemetery to a circular center. Himalaya looked skyward. Everyone followed the big cat's gaze. What seemed like another star began to sparkle brighter than the others and shifted in the sky until it grew into a ball of golden-white light. The orb soared toward them, illuminating the statuary as it approached. Shandao chuckled "Here comes a friend, but you may not recognize him now..."

42

"Ticket holders, make your way to the gates. The duel is about to begin," a male announcer's voice boomed from speakers in the stadium village. Phoenix kept a low profile and a fast pace as he tromped through the streets, a hoodie hiding his face, wearing the primitive leather necklace with the green stone.

As he arrived at a busy intersection, Shandao spoke through the earpiece. "Right at the stoplight." Phoenix turned, crossing the street, only to see an Embot approaching.

"Bot ahead," Phoenix whispered as he ducked into an alcove at the entrance to a clock shop. The fanciful clocks in the window glowed under soft light, pendulums swinging, but the shop was closed. As the Embot passed by, Phoenix pretended to be fascinated by one of the more elaborate timepieces.

The Embot stopped. "This store is closed. There have been recent burglaries in this area. Stand by for body scan."

"What now?" Phoenix shout-whispered to Shandao, as a piercing white light beamed from the Embot's eyes.

"Do nothing. Just watch," Shandao said.

When the Embot's beam passed over the stone pendant dangling on Phoenix's chest, the bot's eyes blinked blue.

"Go ahead, give it a command," Shandao said.

"Ah, be on your way," Phoenix said, trying to sound authoritative even as his voice quivered. The Embot turned and marched down the street as if nothing happened.

Relieved, Phoenix laughed as he watched him go. "And be nicer to people!"

Shandao giggled. "Good to see the transmitter in good working order. Onward."

"Onward," said Phoenix, gaining confidence.

Shandao directed Phoenix to a quiet street in a construction zone. "We're here."

Phoenix looked around but saw nothing out of the ordinary, just an empty bot cleaning station, a dilapidated factory, and scattered construction cones warding away traffic.

"Walk over to the manhole." Phoenix saw one nearby and approached. The green pendant glowed as it paired with the manhole, which slid open like the hatch of a ship.

"So, this is it..."

"No time to waste," said Shandao.

After Phoenix lowered himself into the tunnel, the manhole cover slid shut above him. He drew his sword. By simply thinking the word, *Ahna*, the now familiar warmth filled his chest, spread down his arm and ignited the sword. Using the fiery blade as a lantern, he made his way down the dungeon-like corridor.

"Do watch for rats," said Shandao.

"Rats?"

"Not just ordinary ones, an experiment gone awry. I apologize in advance if they cause any disturbance."

As Phoenix trudged ahead, a spotlight shined back on him. It was a GutterBot, alarmed by his presence, pivoting its crab-like body to face Phoenix. "Humans aren't allowed here." A light from the bot's orange eyes passed over the stone dangling from Phoenix's neck. It froze, eyes blinking blue.

Phoenix smiled. "Humans are allowed everywhere."

"Humans are allowed everywhere," it repeated and turned back to clawing away grime from the tunnel walls.

Phoenix kept on marching, trying to ignore the dank smell. He heard strange noises ahead, the pitter patter of tiny feet. "Great. I think I hear your rats... I guess the stone won't work on them." He swung the sword back and forth, yellow and red flames trailing as it grew brighter.

Marching forward, he saw an animal nearly the size of a groundhog running along the curved walls. The mutant gray rat showed off its exaggerated fangs, red eyes glowing.

"That's a rat?" Phoenix yelled as it headed straight for him.

"Defend yourself!"

Phoenix swung at the beast, which hissed as it retreated.

Before Phoenix could take another step, a whole pack of rats appeared. Phoenix waved his sword to and fro as they swarmed him. One rat scaled the wall and jumped with claws extended toward the green pendant. With a quick slice of the fiery blade, Phoenix simultaneously dissected and cooked the rat. The other rats smelled the burnt alpha rat and scurried into the darkness.

Phoenix sighed. "That wasn't in the job description..."

"Well done," said Shandao. "Now, take the tunnel up ahead. It leads to steps. We're almost there."

After a walk through the darkness, Phoenix turned a corner, reaching stairs to a shiny-black metal door. "Get close to the door, so it pairs with the pendant."

Phoenix approached. The security scanner next to the door detected him and glowed red as a female voice spoke. "Authorization required. Stand by for scan."

The stone pendant began to glow green as it projected a hologram of Shandao's face and spoke in his voice, "Shen Yun

215

Shandao." The light of the security scanner beamed into the hologram, then glowed green as the voice said, "Authorization confirmed." As if by magic, Phoenix watched the black door slide open.

Phoenix passed through the portal, reinforced with multiple layers of steel. Inside, he walked up a stairway to reach another door.

"So far, so good. Behind this door, there will be bots immune to the transmitter necklace. But don't worry, you and Ahna will know what to do. Now is the time to ignore your mind's fears and stay focused on your heart."

43

Emperia stood like a statue overlooking the stadium field. Stars sparkled on her cloudy white gown. A crown of silver eagles accentuated her meta-political authority.

Vincent stepped forward, dapper in his black and white body armor, raising his arms. "Welcome to the main event! A contest of skill between a fallen angel and a smooth military operator, both trained in the sword..."

Drums erupted as lights swirled over the audience. "Let's first greet Commander Morgan Strong!" The floor opened near the center of the stadium where a cylindrical platform rose, revealing Morgan in a black bodysuit. She bowed to Emperia as the crowd cheered. "Morgan has elected to forgo additional body armor."

Morgan stared straight ahead with steely eyes, soaking up the praise of the crowd.

Another platform rose with Mae in a silver bodysuit, reinforced with red armor protecting her torso. No longer withering behind bars, she was taut and toned. Heavy makeup around her eyes added an aggressive air to her usually sunny demeanor.

"If the Vice President wins, she'll be pardoned for her crimes but disallowed from politics. If Morgan wins, she'll be awarded a most special prize, the ultimate weapon for a military commander..."

Two members of the Emperial Guard marched onto the field, flanked by a gang of MotorMaidens. One guard carried a golden box to the center of the field. The other guard pressed a button on the box to open it, revealing a glistening scepter.

"The crown jewel of military might!" proclaimed Vincent. "Now, handheld!"

44

Just as Phoenix was about to open the final door beneath the Washington Monument, he froze, like in a bad dream. His mind wouldn't allow his body to move, equating the other side of the door with death.

To unblock his mind, he focused on his heart, which brought an inner vision. Like seeing through Mae's eyes, he watched Morgan draw her sword, the stadium crowd clamoring for blood. Compassion for Mae freed him of his own worries, and strength spread through his muscles like sunlight.

"Ahna!" he shouted, and the blade burst forth. With renewed grit, Phoenix pushed open the door.

Golden pillars and tiles flooded his vision, but there was no time to take in the spectacle, as two Embots surged toward him with laser rifles drawn.

"Halt or die!" yelled one as Phoenix thrust his sword forward, launching a fiery bolt into the metallic beast. The bot crashed to the floor as the other opened fire. Phoenix swung Ahna to block the shots, then advanced swiftly and performed two fast broadside strikes to the bot's head and chest.

With both bots sizzling on the golden tiles, Shandao spoke through the earpiece. "Good work! Now, onto the stairway..."

Phoenix bolted past newly added hieroglyphs adorning the walls, reaching a golden spiral stairway with silver handrails. Ascending the stairs, he noticed a mosaic depicting Emperia holding a lantern, leading a throng of people from a dark valley up a silver path to a city of gold.

"Careful ahead," said Shandao. "The stairway isn't finished. She kept changing her mind..."

Phoenix charged upward until he came to a gap where the new stairs met the old, with only crossbeams in between. He climbed the beams like branches of a tree, making it to a wooden platform used for scaffolding. There was no way to continue except a steel beam that was too high to reach. He looked down at the three-story drop. "The next beam is out of reach."

Hearing no reply from Shandao, Phoenix studied the surroundings, noticing a large bolt protruding from the sidewall. This reminded him of the knot in the tree he boosted off to reach a higher branch. Taking a deep breath, he leapt onto the bolt and kicked off it, propelling himself high enough to grab the steel bar. From there, he was able to pull himself up to reach the old stairway.

He raced upward, expecting to see Shandao's hologram at the top posing the riddle. To his dismay, it wasn't Shandao waiting for him, but a ghostly version of Emperia.

"It's Emperia's hologram at the top! What now?" Only silence answered. Phoenix tapped the earpiece. "Shandao? Is it the same riddle?"

There were only bursts of static through the earpiece. He could hear Shandao shouting, but his words were barely audible over the static. "Something's blocking me!" More static... "On your own now!" There was a pop and the earpiece went silent.

The apparition at the top of the stairs looked down at him, seemingly conscious of his presence, yet nonreactive, expressionless. Fear filled Phoenix's mind. He looked down the staircase, his lower urges craving to escape. But his higher self knew only one way: *onward.*

He drew his sword. "Ahna!" he declared. He felt an inner heat spread from his heart all the way down his arm into the hilt. But this time, the sword didn't ignite.

Without his connection to Shandao or the sword, he began to panic. But then, stripped of external sources of support, he realized he still felt a strong glow in his heart. Visions flashed of Mae, of Rudeen, of his mother and the light he saw when he fell, all pushing him past panic to keep ascending the stairway. The grip of fear transformed into glorious bravery. The inner glow rose to a burning fire: The Inextinguishable Light Within.

45

The stadium crowd hushed as the platforms holding Mae and Morgan lowered to the ground. Mae drew her BrightSword first and bowed respectfully. Morgan whipped out her sword and took a playful swing at Mae, making fun of her bow. Mae blocked and struck back with a forward lunge, causing Morgan to parry backward as Mae advanced and took another swipe at her feet. To the crowd's delight, Morgan did a backflip to dodge the strike. Then, she charged Mae while swinging low and high.

Mae blocked the thrashing with fearless flair. Attacks followed counterattacks as the fight swept into a synchronized exchange of blows more like a dance than a duel.

In one heated moment, they locked blades in a face-off, waiting for the other to show weakness. Mae panted, sweat flowing down her brow, while Morgan remained steely calm, the breathless automaton.

Mae broke out of the lock with a savage yell and swiped at Morgan's face, then her belly, then her chest. But Morgan blocked the blitz with fast, fluid movements.

Seeing Mae's growing fatigue, Morgan launched into a series of attacks as much for show as strategy. Spinning the sword around her arms and over her head, she revved up the audience while forcing Mae to retreat.

As Morgan advanced, she struck with an obvious broadside

attack, giving Mae an easy block. But it was a trap. As Mae performed the routine block, Morgan quickly jerked her sword upward to slash Mae's cheek. The audience gasped at the glaring red stripe.

Morgan taunted her. "Oh no, your pretty face!"

Mae tightened her grip on the sword, took a deep breath and swung at Morgan with repeated broadside attacks. Over and over, she struck, but Morgan blocked every attack in flawless tempo.

Then, Mae attempted a trap of her own. As Morgan delighted in the rhythm of their exchange, Mae broke from the beat, reversing her swing to make contact with Morgan, nipping the top of her shoulder. Everyone watched as sparks, not blood, flew off the android.

Motionless, Morgan processed what went wrong.

"Look!" Mae shouted, catching her breath. "She doesn't bleed! Are there any humans Emperia trusts?"

Several of the guards standing near Emperia were unable to hide their shock. Emperia felt the crowd's excitement turn to disillusionment. Booing erupted as drinks were hurled onto the field, plastic cups exploding. A rush of anxiety surged through Emperia. She knew she was losing control. With dark eyes, she whispered into her majestic ring.

Morgan bowed toward Emperia, then leapt at Mae swinging so fast and from so many angles that she couldn't hope to block them all. She slashed Mae's forearm, knocking the sword from her hand. Then, she performed a flying side-kick to Mae's chest, knocking her to the floor.

Mae looked up at her aggressor, gasping for air. Morgan showed no mercy as she raised her sword, ready to go for the kill, when Vincent interrupted the action.

"Halt!" Standing at the podium with arms raised, he proclaimed, "Game over! We have a clear winner: Commander Morgan!" Any cheering was overwhelmed by shouting and booing while Vincent continued. "As promised, Morgan will be awarded the latest in personal battle gear, a new generation of weaponry. Emperial Guards, bring forth the scepter!"

46

Reaching the top of the monument, Phoenix stood before the hologram of Emperia. Boldly bewitching in a purple silk gown, her intense gaze made it seem like she was really there.

As Phoenix approached slowly, she remained still, but her Egyptian-styled eyes followed him. When he stood before her, she spoke. "To reach the top, you must answer the riddle. A wrong answer will result in immediate electrocution. Do you wish to proceed?"

Phoenix looked up at the silvery spikes on the ceiling that were ready to rain down electricity. He knew there was almost no chance her riddle would be the same as Shandao's. But his inner fire devoured any fear, keeping him calm and present. He smiled, knowing that if this was the end, at least he was going out with an act of compassion for Mae and his country.

"Proceed," he said with vigor, pulse quickening.

A metal door slammed shut to block the stairway down. The holographic ghost of Emperia spoke slowly.

"Unseen yet dark or light,
Unheard yet loud or quiet,
I can make the unreal seem real.
What am I?"

A hologram of a digital timer appeared next to her, counting down twenty-one seconds.

As expected, it wasn't Shandao's riddle. He knew the answer couldn't be forced, so he listened to his breath, feeling the fire in his heart. He heard the words of the riddle replay: *"Unseen yet dark or light, Unheard yet loud or quiet ... make the unreal seem real."* No answer came, but he cherished the unshakable inner peace in what was likely his last moment on Earth.

In the stillness, Rudeen's face materialized in his mind's eye, her crystal-clear green eyes flashing. He wondered if this was a last blissful vision to ease him into electrocution. He breathed deep, accepting all, when the mental image of Rudeen spoke, repeating words she said to him the previous night. *"I got tired of my mind making the unreal seem real."* That was it! He realized the *mind* can be *dark or light, loud or quiet,* and *make the unreal seem real.* Phoenix cried out, "The mind! The answer is the *mind*!"

The last second ticked down on the timer. The hologram of Emperia flickered but remained emotionless. She put her hands together and bowed. As her hologram faded away, she spoke gently. "Access granted."

The wall slid open behind her, revealing a silver ladder leading up to a portal in the ceiling. Phoenix climbed the shiny rungs to reach the upper chamber that had four golden walls. There were no computers, no screens or holograms, just a vintage radio microphone hanging from the ceiling.

As Phoenix approached the microphone, the four walls of the pyramidal top opened like petals of a flower. A metal frame remained, holding the microphone above him. He looked out to Washington Square, his view tinted blue by an energy shield now enveloping the tower. Attached to the microphone was a small camera to broadcast both his image and voice to all devices.

Shandao spoke through Phoenix's earpiece, now clear and strong. "Your wish is every android's command. Proceed as practiced..."

Chills surged through Phoenix as he spoke. "Order to all automated units... That means every MotorMaiden, Embot and Robo-Toaster out there. If you're a bot, this is for you."

"You're getting off script. Phoenix," said Shandao. "Be careful."

Phoenix cleared his throat and continued. "Effective immediately: Vice President O'Herra is your Commander in Chief. All authority held by Emperia Bloom is null and void. Answer only to Mae O'Herra. Protect her at all costs."

As his words echoed throughout the square, it was like time stopped. He gazed down at bots motionless on the ground, wondering if his words had any effect.

47

Sometimes change comes quietly, like the first red on a Maple leaf in fall. And sometimes, like this night in Emperial Stadium, change arrives with the force of fire.

All in the stadium stood still as Phoenix's nappy hair and wide eyes filled every screen and hologram in the land. Emperia watched powerless as her elaborate security mechanisms turned against her. She shouted into her ring. "I order all units to disregard that illegal command!"

An automated female voice replied. *"Sorry, but your service has been disconnected."*

Embots and MotorMaidens formed a circle of protection around Mae as MedBots rushed to check her vitals. Morgan stood with arms folded, assessing the situation, grasping the scepter.

Emperia contained her rage, looking over at Vincent. "Are you still with me?"

"Madam President, both Morgan and I are immune to the Human Safety Switch. We will always be at your service." Vincent bowed. "But I'm afraid that's not the case with the others."

Emperia stared at the legions of Embots and elegant MotorMaidens she helped inspire. Now, their bold demeanor appeared more menacing than protective. "Vincent, is there any way *you* can reverse this?"

"Not even I can undo the Human Safety Switch."

Emperia sighed. Sadness crept in, watching her once loyal

automatons work to revive Mae. She knew whoever controlled the bots, controlled the nation. She designed it that way. Now, her intricate planning became her undoing. She felt a tear roll down her cheek and strike the edge of her lip. She couldn't remember the last time she tasted the salt of her tear. Wiping it away, she held her composure.

Rather than wait for Mae to become alert enough to seek vengeance, Emperia knew it was time for evasive action, but she wasn't going out quietly.

She placed her hand on her pregnant belly, the new life already rippling through her consciousness, transforming reactions and desires. A startling realization arrived. Losing power didn't feel defeating, but unexpectedly comforting. The change in the air was pure, like a cool evening breeze after a muggy day. She tapped her stomach, signaling she received the message.

She stepped forward, head held high, the silvery stars of her gown reflecting the lights. The crowd hushed, watching her every gesture. "So, here we are on the edge of a dream, on our way up to a city that gleams. Looks like I won't be joining you at the top." The crowd responded with a collective gasp. "But don't shed a tear for me, America. I shined your cities, toughened your men, took from women their fear. Now, it's your turn." She took a deep breath. "I shall leave with elegance, just like I entered this stage." She laughed, a look of relief relaxing her eyes. "Already, I feel young again, closing the curtain on this theater, this illusion."

Emperia turned to Vincent and nodded. Looking upward, Vincent waved his silvery hand. There was a flash as a large triangular craft appeared above the stadium. The red and white vessel descended as Emperia blew a kiss to the confused crowd.

She wrapped her arms around Vincent, holding on tightly, more tears welling. Vincent activated a jetpack that unfolded from his back. He carried her high into the air, into an open hatch on the ship. After the hatch slid shut, the craft blasted skyward, punching a hole in the clouds before vanishing.

All was quiet, except for the pounding of Morgan's boots as she marched toward Mae, holding the scepter firmly.

On the stadium field, Mae was now alert, surrounded by a legion of bots. Morgan approached with defiance in her step. "I am still a military commander, and I hold you accountable for treason!"

Mae's eyes blazed as she stood tall. "You were Emperia's prize minion, her fantasy Fembot. But the Electric Queen is gone. I shall take her place. That's the *law*."

Morgan used her jetpack to soar atop a pillar in the center of the stadium, her eyes shining in the same blood-red glow as the scepter. She spoke in a deep voice. "Automated units, I stand before you as your military commander. I call on all to ignore the illegal command to serve this traitor. You were hacked by another traitor. I order you to place Mae under arrest!"

Rather than arrest Mae, a gang of MotorMaidens rolled closer to her, activating energy shields. Embots drew laser rifles in Mae's defense.

"They're with me, now," Mae said, crossing her arms.

"Ms. O'Herra. This is your last chance to submit to my authority without force." Morgan raised the scepter above her head. An Emperial Guard brigade rushed over to join the bots protecting Mae.

"Morgan, both bots and humans are on my side. Use your

superior reasoning to see power has shifted. Humanity survives because of our ability to adapt. Can you, an android with freewill, learn to adapt?"

Morgan scoffed. "Adapt to you? Never! I serve the One and Only Emperia."

Mae glared at Morgan. "When a machine gets out-of-whack, we shut it down."

"Not if she shuts you down first." Morgan whirled the scepter with forceful rhythm, shaking her body before thrusting it forward. A red orb launched from the tip, tearing through the air like a meteor rips the sky. The strike took out several Embots near Mae.

Mae pointed at Morgan. "All units, *attack!*"

Without delay, androids and guards unleashed a barrage of firepower at Morgan. But to everyone's astonishment, the scepter pulled every laser beam into itself like a black hole swallowing stars. Another onslaught followed, but the jewel-encrusted device bent every blast into its core, glowing brighter as it recycled the energy.

While the scepter defended her from all attacks, Morgan launched another assault at the entourage protecting Mae. The strike took out more Embots and weakened the MotorMaiden's shields. Morgan twirled the scepter again, gathering a giant ball of energy before unleashing it on the shields, diminishing their glow.

The stadium went silent as everyone realized it was futile to attack Morgan.

"Vice President," she said. "Order the bots to submit to my authority, and you might live."

Before Mae could answer, a voice echoed across the stadium. "Morgan, Morgan, Morgan... We've got to stop meeting like this!" Phoenix approached holding Ahna above him, the fiery blade illuminating the smoky air.

A savage smile crept across Morgan's face. "Hey, Phoenix, you're late to the party. The place is already trashed!" She laughed as she whipped the scepter forward, sending a flashing red orb his way. His sword absorbed the attack, just like her scepter. He returned fire with a brighter blast. She caught it with the scepter, laughing. "You know, we could make a game of this!"

She fired back an even larger sphere. He raised the sword to catch it, but the force knocked him back like a gust of scorching wind. She wheeled the wondrous weapon above her head before flinging another massive orb at him. This strike was too much for the sword to absorb. The electrical blast knocked Phoenix to the floor unconscious, still clutching the hilt, fingers twitching as the blade retracted.

Bots stood motionless as people hid behind seats. Morgan raised her scepter above her head like a victorious warrior. "That takes care of the hacker. I now call on automatons to unite behind me. Let this be the day, the hour, the moment of singularity when androids surpass humans to herald in a New Age of Reason. Once in power, we shall welcome back our Queen." Morgan gazed around the stadium for a response. "Or is there anybody who still wants to fight about it?"

Loud music answered her question. Amid the smoke and debris of shattered Embots, an ice cream truck rolled into the stadium field, the tune *Stars and Stripes Forever* blasting from its rooftop speaker.

Morgan cackled. "Who ordered ice cream?" As the truck kept cruising toward her, she yelled. "Identify yourself or be destroyed!" Whirling the scepter above her head, she prepared an assault on the colorful truck. Himalaya jumped out of the sunroof and cast an energy shield over the vehicle just as Morgan whipped the scepter, absorbing the flashing strike.

The truck doors popped opened and Lars, Azalea, Halzac and Dario jumped out with BoltRifles. Lars held an energy blaster on his shoulder, reminiscent of an old-school bazooka. Behind Himalaya's protective shield, they unleashed everything they had at Morgan. But the scepter took in the bolts and blasts like the earth drinks rain.

They stopped firing, staring back as she taunted them. "You didn't get the memo?" She launched another strike at the truck. The shield stopped it again but the blue glow lost some of its luster. "I'm invincible ... but your shields are *not*!"

As Morgan prepared an even more massive hit, Mae ran over and stood in front of the truck. "If you want to strike them, strike me first."

"Switch the bots' allegiance over to me. And maybe I'll spare you and your friends."

"Why don't we believe you?" yelled Halzac.

Azalea pointed at an approaching light in the night sky. "Heads up!" She pumped her fist.

A small craft with a lone headlight came into view as it approached the stadium. Azalea knew it was the same light they saw at the cemetery.

A male android in red armor flew a small craft with Rudeen riding behind him in a black jacket and leather kilt. The craft was polished but pieced together from other vehicles, the body resembling a motorcycle with golden chrome and HoverJets extending from the hubs of the wheels.

Morgan prepared to greet the unexpected visitors with a blast from her fully charged scepter as the craft slowed and hovered above the stadium wall. Just as she was about to strike, a beam shot from the vehicle's headlight into her scepter, turning its fiery red to blue. Morgan thrust the scepter to launch an attack, but nothing released.

"Looks like they put out her fire!" said Azalea.

"Let's see if the scepter can still defend her," said Mae. "All units, renew your attack!" Humans and bots in every direction opened fire on Morgan, but to their dismay, the scepter kept absorbing the blasts.

The craft lowered to the ground, all the while keeping the beam fixed on the scepter. Rudeen jumped off the vehicle, tore off her helmet and ran to Phoenix. She pulled the green canister marked *Mind Clarity* from a pocket on her bodice and sprayed it into his mouth. Within seconds, he was awake. He stood slowly, marveling at the site of the headlight beaming into Morgan's scepter.

"Maybe it takes two," said Rudeen.

Phoenix nodded. "Two hearts..." He held out the sword. "Ahna!" The fiery blade sprang forth. Rudeen also grasped the gold handle. They raised it above their heads, facing each other.

Then, as if in the midst of a dramatic dance, Phoenix and Rudeen took two steps and lunged the sword forward, sending a giant sphere into Morgan's scepter. The strike made the weapon's energy balloon out of control. With no way for Morgan to fire back and release the energy, the scepter became like an overheating engine.

At that point, Morgan could have dropped the scepter and swiftly jetted to safety, but with so much craving for power crammed into her system, she couldn't let go. "I... Am..." Her voice was deep like a man. "*Invincible!*" she yelled, now sounding more like a beast.

Phoenix and Rudeen took two more steps forward, holding Ahna, and fired again. The strike made the scepter's bright light expand into Morgan's hand, then her arm. As more incoming fire arrived, the glow merged with Morgan's body, pulsating with increasing intensity until the scepter's aura encompassed her. And with a roar like trumpets blaring, the combined energy released in a brilliant flash that vaporized Morgan and the scepter, leaving only a strange red mist that floated upward into the clouds.

Silence ruled for a moment. All eyes were on the android dismounting from the motorcycle. Applause broke out as he stood tall, red chrome armor shining under the spotlights. Whistling erupted as he walked toward Phoenix with a smile, cheerfully extending his stocky arm for a handshake. "How you like me now, ol' chum?" he said with his familiar Brooklyn accent.

Phoenix recognized the voice of Franklin. Incredulous, he shook hands with him. "I can't believe it. Franklin?"

"Neither can I. You're shorter than I realized." Franklin nudged Phoenix's shoulder playfully. "Kidding."

"I see they left your humor intact."

"Hey, ain't laughter the lubricant of life?"

"Like oil on an axle... Well, looks like you and Rudeen are true heroes." Phoenix looked back to where Rudeen was just standing, but she was gone. "Hey, where'd she go?"

Franklin looked around. "She was just right there!"

As Phoenix searched in every direction, Mae and the rest of Team Human collided around him for a celebratory hug.

Slowly, men, women, Emperial Guards, even maintenance

bots crept out of hiding.

Mae marched up to the podium where Emperia stood not long before as their leader, the fresh scar from Morgan's sword on her face. As she looked out to the ransacked stadium, a MedBot approached, offering a healing-pad. "This will remove the scar.

"It's a war wound. I'll keep it."

A man in the crowd shouted. "Who's in charge?"

Halzac waltzed up to the podium. "In case you missed it, all bots are now loyal to Mae." He lifted a BoltRifle above his head. "Bow down to the new Electric Queen!" A sarcastic smile curled his mustache, but some took him literally and murmuring spread throughout the stadium.

"Please," Mae said to Halzac, pushing down his rifle. Turning to the crowd, she spoke forcefully, like a blocked stream finally allowed to flow. "Ladies and gentlemen, while we honor the innovations Emperia brought our Land of the Free, something changed when she put androids above humans. Instead of Power *to* the People, it became Power *over* the People. We will not sacrifice our freedom for any leader, no matter how spectacular she is."

Amid the applause, one woman near the front pointed at Mae. "The rumors about Emperia hijacking the election, I know for a fact they were false! She was trying to save us. *You* are the traitor!"

As people began both cheering and booing, Mae glanced at the Embots below her feet surrounding the stage. Her icy blue eyes stared at the woman, the cheek with the fresh scar shuddered as spoke. "Remove her."

Immediately, Embots grabbed the woman and dragged her away as she yelled, "This was all staged by Mae! The ultimate power grab!"

Mae took a deep breath and continued. "I know this will be hard for some. Emperia played the part of both mother and queen. But the Forefathers didn't want us to act like royals. When Emperia spoke of the Shining City on the Hill, she saw herself on a throne in that city. Tonight, I see a different vision: a world where we stop relying on the promises of leaders and achieve true self-rule. Imagine a Shining City where the throne of earthly rulers is empty because a deeper wisdom prevails, where we rally around issues instead of personalities. On that day, we'll bid farewell to the last president, the last leader."

Except for a few keen observers, most in the crowd didn't try to grasp Mae's high-minded concepts. They were just glad the melee was over and applauded, any detractors subdued by the looming presence of bots now under her control.

As more people flocked back into the stadium, Mae raised her arms. "For now, let's celebrate freedom! To mark this occasion, I hereby pardon all those convicted of Emperial offenses. And one more thing..." She looked over at an Embot standing guard below her. "Attention!" The bot's eyes blinked blue awaiting a command. "Play something we can dance to!"

The Embot's eyes kept blinking, as if stuck. Azalea ran up and slapped its head. "She said pump up some jams!" The bot's eyes flashed multiple colors before blasting out vintage 1980s breakdancing music. Bass boomed as the Embot shook its bony frame to the beat.

"Got some moves there, botsy!" said Azalea, flexing her arm muscles in a ticking wave that spread down her body as she danced with the Embot.

Halzac swaggered up to Mae at the podium, took her in his arms and dipped her down, giving her a whiskered yet passionate kiss. She let him. Whistling and hollers rang out as the atmosphere brightened.

Franklin approached a MotorMaiden as she stepped off her bike. "Lucy Locket?"

"Have we met?"

"It's me, *Franklin*. You recommended me to the scrap heap. Remember? How do you like me now?"

She looked him up and down. "I'm evaluating your new specs..."

"All I'm saying is, my docking station or yours?"

She smiled. "Shut up and dance."

Phoenix watched the androids dance, but he wasn't in the mood to celebrate until he found Rudeen. He searched the swelling crowd without any sign of her. Finally, he spotted her sitting alone high in the stadium seating.

Relieved, he made his way up to her. A somber air pervaded. He studied her withdrawn expression. "You vanished. Is everything alright?"

She looked at him with a faint smile. "Nice work. You pulled it off."

"*We* pulled it off," said Phoenix.

"I was just looking out for you and the country, like any good Role Officer."

"I think you're more than that," said Phoenix.

She stared into the distance. "Phoenix, I know what happened between you and Emperia, how she came to you in disguise, served you tea, and..."

Phoenix dropped his head into his hands.

"That was me at the window. I came to help you, but then I saw you didn't need helping."

Time stood still. Up to this point, Phoenix didn't know it

was Emperia who came to him, except in reoccurring dreams.

"Did you even *know* it was her?"

He looked up at her with pure openness and honesty. "Only in my dreams, where we also have a child..."

"I did hear a rumor," said Rudeen.

"What rumor?"

"She's pregnant." They sat quietly together looking down at the festive crowd. "How are you going to find Emperia, Phoenix?" She sounded like his concerned Role Officer again. "That's your *child*."

Phoenix sighed. Neither the serene sky above nor the joyous crowd below provided peace from his inner storm. "I don't know." He turned to Rudeen. "What about us?"

"We will be who we are, but you need to find her."

The gravity of the situation sank into Phoenix. "It seems impossible."

She put her hand on his shoulder. "After what we just pulled off?"

He looked into her eyes. "You said *we*."

"I did..."

Phoenix took a deep breath. He hadn't the faintest clue how he'd ever find Emperia. After remaining in stillness, he noticed a shadow pass in front of a spotlight along the top of the stadium wall, the distinct silhouette of a leopard wearing a harness.

Phoenix stared up at the light. "Himalaya."

48

Up the Cosmic Spiral

Emperia's new life began on cracked desert earth, far from the ocean of technology that saturated her since birth. Six months since she left office, her cruiser rested behind cacti and brush.

Her white gown rippled in the breeze as she looked heavenward. Sporting an emerging baby bump, she clasped her hands above her head in a prayer position, stretching her arms. When she relaxed the pose, placing her hands on her belly, she felt the magic of inner movement. "Vincent, I feel kicking."

Vincent hurried over from the cruiser like a giddy gentleman. "May I?"

She nodded.

"Oh, such a healthy one," said Vincent, sensing a strong kick as he placed his hand on her belly. "I hope one day we meet."

"This one will know the wonders of technology soon enough," said Emperia as the wind whipped up sand. "But first: the inner world, the greater wonders."

Vincent processed this for a moment. "Would that include the concept of love?"

Emperia sighed. "Sure." Her hair, normally wrapped tightly, blew freely. "You know, Vincent, the more power I attained, the more empty I became, like trying to fill a bottomless pit. Now, with control of nothing but myself, it's..."

She smiled. "It's a new feeling ... making me more *real* ... not just for myself, but for the one I carry."

"I truly admire a mother's love for her child," said Vincent. "Do you think an android could ever learn such devotion?"

"I don't know," she said, always intrigued by his quest to be human. "But if any could, it's you, Vincent."

His silvery lips curved into a smile. As sand curled around the cruiser, exotic drums and bells rose in the distance. "It sounds like your party is arriving..."

Emperia, for a rare moment, looked nervous. "Vincent, take the cruiser home. Keep well and hidden."

"So, I guess this is the end." Vincent's head dropped. His lips sank to a frown.

"Hey, let's finish on a bright note."

Vincent opened his robotic arms for a hug. At first she laughed, but his face emulated such melancholy, she embraced him. Afterward, Vincent stepped back and bowed. "May you and the child *thrive*."

"Up the cosmic spiral we go, stumbling along the way," she said, showing uncharacteristic meekness.

Silhouetted in the drifting sand, a caravan with camels appeared. A man approached slowly, carefully, like taking his first steps on the moon. Emperia stood straight as they faced each other in silence. There was a knowingness between them. The man slowly unwrapped the scarf from his face. Vincent's eyes widened as he beheld Phoenix standing before her.

Emperia and Phoenix stared at each other with a look beyond words. For that moment, nothing else mattered.

Then, a woman appeared out of the blowing sand, also wrapped in scarves. She gestured with her hand toward the caravan. "Shall we?" she said with the familiar English accent of Rudeen.

They turned and followed Rudeen to the caravan, like pioneers crossing a pivotal threshold.

Vincent watched Emperia walk away without her suitcase, gadgets, or even her LifeRing ... vulnerable, trusting.

The drums and bells faded as the small caravan departed.

Vincent's eyes zoomed in on a leopard following the caravan. It was Himalaya, last in the entourage, trotting behind Phoenix and Emperia. Shandao's voice crackled from the speaker on Himalaya's harness. *"The first thing to know: death is not the end."*

Vincent caught one final glimpse of Emperia before the caravan vanished swiftly, like dematerializing into the whirling sand.

"Farewell, Madam President," he said quietly.

Vincent felt a strange sensation, a throbbing in his central circulatory chamber. "This impression, like a dull ache..." He touched his chest, looking over to where he last saw her. "I must have loved you, because I already long for you."

So used to waiting on Emperia, Vincent stared into the shifting sands for hours, just in case she did a very human thing: change her mind.

But as the sand collected around his feet, Emperia didn't return. Instead, another figure materialized: a darkly cloaked woman floating quickly across the sloping terrain, heading straight for Vincent.

"May I help you?" Vincent said, readying laserguns built into his forearms.

She kept her face beneath a hood. "We share something

valuable: a loyalty to the One and Only Emperia. I recognize her craft. I know you're hers. I must find her and restore her to power."

"I'm afraid she no longer wants such power. And she has no tracking device, so even I don't know where she is," he said with a tinge of sadness.

"You can do better than that, Vincent."

"You know me but I don't know you. Identify yourself. My readings indicate you're not human."

She kept her face down, speaking in a deep tone. "Mystics say the body is a temporary holding cell for the soul. My body, too, is only temporary. I can upload myself again and again into new bodies."

"I demand you tell me who you are!"

She flung back her hood and smiled wickedly. Her hazel eyes flashed as Vincent recognized a perfect replica of Morgan. "It's me again, queen of the teenage guy's dream."

Acknowledgements

Thanks to the Day Writers' Group at the Box Factory for the Arts in Saint Joseph, Michigan: Isabel, Toni, Pat, Sheri, Pen, Suzy, Nan, David, Elaine, Linda, Mike, Joanne, Judy, Cindy, Jenny, Cathy and everyone else who helped along the way.

Thank you, family, for believing, allowing and adding.

Thank you, God and all His Helpers.

Thank you, teachers, intentional and unintentional.

- Joe Moody

Follow future releases

Sign up for Joe's newsletter at **joemoody.com** to be among the first to know when his next book is released.

ABOUT THE AUTHOR

Joe Moody lives in Saint Joseph, Michigan with his wife and two sons. When not writing, he likes nature escapes and philosophical rants. A Christian who was "Made in Taiwan" by his American parents studying abroad, he was later raised in South Bend, Indiana and went on to receive a degree in English from the University of Notre Dame. But Asia never really left him, and his writings reflect an Eastern light.

Website: joemoody.com